MOUNTED

BITTERSWEET FARM 1

MOUNTED

Barbara Morgenroth

DASHINGBOOKS

ISBN 978-0-6158729-9-5

Cover photo by Sommer Wilson

Published by DashingBooks

Text set in Adobe Garamond

— 1 —

THE AIR WAS SHIMMERING with the oppressive heat on the late June morning. The weekend show was over and our horses had a day off, but Greer didn't. I looked at my half-sister in the hay and said, "You might want to stop what you're doing. Dad's on his way."

* * *

I took a sip of my iced tea. "Yes. Greer does the unbelievable all the time."

"What did your father say?"

"After all the yelling? 'You're fired'."

Rogers dipped a French fry in the catsup on her plate. "Talia, now you don't have a trainer."

"That's the least of my worries," I replied. "I could barely understand the Portuguese accent anyway."

"If that's the least," Rogers said, "what's the biggest?"

"I'm going to be dragged to a horse show every weekend until Greer qualifies for the Maclay."

"She hasn't yet?"

"Maybe she would have if Nicole Boisvert wasn't at all the same shows, wasn't just a little bit better and had a horse who managed to stay sound all spring."

"Go somewhere else, another state."

"Rui had a plan for her."

"I guess," Rogers said, then laughed. "I can't believe she was . . ."

"Don't go there."

"It was a bit weird hiring a Brazilian to be your trainer."

"He came well-recommended. Rui was short-listed for the Olympic team."

Rogers used a paper napkin to wipe her lips, crumpled it up and dropped it onto her plate. "How many is this?"

I had to think for a moment. "Six."

"Are you counting that woman from Canada?"

"I forgot her."

"I'm sure your father thought she'd be a safe bet."

"That's why Greer made her life miserable and ran her off. It doesn't matter who is next, we all know what's going to happen."

Greer was like her father. Energetic in all he did. Since

that was the truth and he knew it, it was hard to complain about her behavior. He tried once but she just threw the truth back in his face and ever since other methods were employed to keep Greer on a leash. It was all as inevitable as a horse rolling in the dirt after a bath.

"What about you?"

"Horse shows are a major bore."

"Stop going."

I stood and put money on the table for my share of the bill. "I tried that once. Just once. I have to get home."

My father didn't have so much of a temper as a command. When he said something, he meant it and I never wanted to test him.

"Call me later."

I nodded, opened the door to the café and walked out onto the uneven sidewalk of Newbury. In front of me was the Green; at the north end there was a fountain and at the south end a War memorial statue surrounded by a bed of red geraniums maintained by the local garden club. In the autumn, sheaves of corn would be brought in. In the winter, there would be fairy lights, large red ribbons on the lamp posts and a tree-lighting ceremony with Christmas carols. In the spring, the grass would be brown and the ground would be muddy.

This typical historic New England village had been my home for the past six years but it still didn't feel like it. It was more like being on an extended excursion with people you didn't know very well, didn't want to know and just wanted to go home.

There was no going home again.

Getting in my pickup truck, I sat there for several minutes before turning the key in the ignition. I lived on an eight hundred acre estate in Litchfield County, Connecticut, if I wanted anything, and I did not, all I had to do was ask and it would be mine and I didn't want to drive back there.

It was easy to understand why Mellissa left after ten days. I'd leave if it was possible. Greer would drive anyone off. The only reason why she didn't start on me was that she simply didn't hate me. In some ways, I improved her life by making her look like an excellent rider instead of just a good one. The added bonus was that I made her the most desirable girl in school. As hot as she was, I was perceived to be cold. The only thing a guy could expect to get from me if he tried anything was a boot to the groin.

I reversed the truck out of the parking space and headed back to Bittersweet Farm.

* * *

"This was an exciting afternoon, wasn't it?" Jules said as she sautéed the onions, celery and carrots in a pan.

I sat on one of the tall stools next to the island. "Do you understand it?"

"Excuse me?"

"Greer. Why she does these things? Is it one of those things adults always say you'll understand once you're older?"

Jules laughed. "No." She diced a fresh tomato and added it to the baking dish. "I'm not that much older than you are, Tal, and I don't understand her."

Jules was the live-in chef. She had been to France to study cooking and after deciding that working in a restaurant was too hectic, working for this household would be so much more relaxing. I couldn't imagine how she arrived at that conclusion but she seemed happy here.

"Is the girlfriend home?"

"She's in the city shopping and then staying at the apartment so she can continue shopping tomorrow."

"I guess it must be close to over."

Jules shrugged. "I couldn't say."

That's what they all did—loaded up on the trinkets at Tiffany's and Manolo Blahnik's before my father pulled the plug on their credit cards. He was generous or glad to get rid of them with a nice settlement and introductions to other men who might wind up marrying them if they got lucky.

* * *

"Your new coach is arriving the day after tomorrow," my father announced at dinner.

"Okay," I replied.

5

"This time we're going to be doing things a little bit differently."

"He's a eunuch?" I asked.

"Shut up," Greer snapped.

"You may have heard of him. Lockie Malone."

Not as famous as one of the Jonas Brothers but everyone on the show circuit had at least heard of Lockie Malone even if he was from California.

He had the reputation of being a wunderkind. Everyone knew the only thing that held him back as a junior rider was money. The last I heard was he had found a rich benefactor in Santa Barbara and was riding for him. I think that man had daughters, too.

"Aren't you lucky, Greer," I said to her.

"Shut up."

* * *

Jules and I were out on the back patio having raspberry lemonade and almond shortbread when a pickup truck and horse trailer drove down to the barn and stopped.

"That must be him," she said. "That's a day early, isn't it?"

"He drove in too fast to have a horse in the trailer so maybe that has something to do with it," I replied.

He got out of his truck and walked into the barn.

Everyone was gone for the afternoon. Jules and I were it.

Greer was in Millbrook at her friend's stable, and Pavel had gone to the hardware store in town.

A moment later, he exited from the barn and glanced around the property. There weren't even horses out in the heat of the day.

"We're up at the house," Jules called and gave me a look.

"I don't want anything to do with him."

"You're stuck with him."

"Until Greer gets too familiar with him and then we'll have another new trainer."

Lockie Malone approached.

"Tal, he's really attractive," Jules said softly to me.

"Don't even dream of it."

"Are you insane? I like it here. The two words I don't want to hear from your father are 'you're fired'."

"Hi," he said as he stepped up into the shade of the stone patio and removed his sunglasses. "I'm Lockie Malone."

As could be predicted, he was tall, lean, and quite tan. The dark hair and blue eyes made a winning lotto ticket.

Jules looked at me again. "Sit down and have some lemonade and shortbread cookies." She reached for a spare glass and the pitcher to pour the icy drink.

He pulled out a chair and sat. "Where is everyone?"

"Are you a day early?"

"Yes. Is that a problem?"

"Greer will be disappointed since she was on your welcoming committee."

"And you are . . ."

I glanced at Jules. "Talia Margolin."

"The other sister."

"Well, we all experience these surprises of fate which impact our lives forever. Make that half-sister."

He smiled and took a cookie from the platter Jules held out. "Your father said you'd like to be called Talia."

I believed in strangers treating me as if they didn't know me because they didn't. "That's fine. And you're the new cruise director."

"You liked Rui better than me?"

"No."

"Then there's hope for me."

"It's Greer's MO to like the trainer in her special way."

Lockie laughed. "Yes. I heard about it. It's the talk of the entire East Coast show circuit."

Beyond being embarrassed by anything Greer did, I pushed back from the table. "Your apartment is over the barn. I'm sure you'll be able to find it."

"You're not going to give me a guided tour?"

"No."

"Okay. I'm sure I can poke around and find everything I need. Your first riding lesson will be tomorrow at nine."

"I'll see you before then."

"Why?"

"Dinner."

"The help eats with the family?"

I glared at him. "Julietta is a first class chef."

Jules held out her hand. "Jules is sufficient and you're welcome to eat with us for every meal."

He reached out and shook her hand.

"Enjoy it while you're here," I said standing up. "You won't be staying that long."

Lockie laughed as I went back into the house.

2

GOING UP THE BACKSTAIRS, I continued down the hall-way to my bedroom where I lay on the bed. If I called Greer to say he had arrived, she'd drive home even faster than normal.

She wanted a Porsche so that's what she got and drove as though every road was the Autobahn. I asked for a used pickup truck but my father got me a new one. "You don't want to buy other people's trouble."

Not in this family where we were perfectly capable of creating our own trouble, thanks.

My cell phone rang and I pulled it out of my pocket. It was Rogers.

"Hi. Do you want to go to the movies tonight?"

"Why didn't you mention it earlier?"

"I just found out. They're running *Après-Midi Étoiles* at the Thaden Theater."

"Is it another French art film from the 1960s?"

"Yes! They're so sensual, so sexy, so adult."

"So boring."

"Please, Tal."

"Not tonight."

"Why not?"

"Lockie Malone showed up a day early."

"Are you kidding me?! What's he like?"

"He won't last the month."

Rogers gasped. "He's that cute?"

"Oh, yeah. Greer will be on him like a foxhound on a scent."

"Can I come over?"

"Yes. You can pick up me for the movie around dinner and see him probably for the first and last time."

"Has Greer seen him yet?"

"She's in Millbrook, so no, she's not home. I was just wondering if I should call her or let it be a surprise."

* * *

Two hours later my door was flung open.

"You bitch!" Greer shouted at me.

"What now?" I didn't look up from the ebook I was reading.

"Lockie Malone arrived and you didn't call me?"

I put the reader in my lap. "I called. Did you check your voice mail?"

She paused.

"Right. Well, you look beautiful after your day at the spa. Put on something nice so he can't resist you and then we can get onto the next trainer. Hopefully that one will be old and wrinkled and last more than a week."

Greer paused in the doorway. "Is he cute?"

"Very handsome; I'm sure you'll find him extremely agreeable."

After a day at the spa, she had new blond highlights in her shoulder length hair that gold earrings would complement perfectly. Greer sparkled in the sun, not like me. I had dark brown hair and brown eyes and if miles away from my half-sister, I could be considered pretty enough. But Greer was born to be the center of attention and she sought it out.

My father encouraged her. He encouraged me, too, but it didn't do much good. I was immune to anonymous praise.

Greer had always adored going to horse shows. The idea of all eyes being on her was like an aphrodisiac and she blossomed with the attention.

I liked to ride but didn't want to compete, especially not against Greer because the outcome was predictable. Yet every year, I found myself at the same shows in the same classes with Greer pinning above me. Part of the reason was that she held no allegiance or affection for any horse and could switch them every season for a newer, shinier model. I was still riding the same horse given me the year my mother died. If I had to attend the shows against my will, at least I wanted to do it with my best friend.

Greer's shower ran and ran while I picked out an oxford shirt and trousers to wear to dinner. We didn't change for lunch unless there were guests, but dinner had other rules, clean and neat being at the top of the list. I gave my hair a quick brush, pulled it back into a clip and went downstairs to the dining room.

Jules entered with the salad. "It's just the three of us."

"Why?"

"Lockie called and said he apologized but after the long drive from Kentucky, he wanted to end the day early. He'll see you in the morning."

"It doesn't make sense," I replied, sitting down. "There's nothing to eat over there."

"I sent a basket over with Pavel."

Greer came into the room and looked around in confusion. "Where is he?"

"You'll have to wait till tomorrow," I replied.

"I got all dressed up for nothing?"

Jules patted Greer's arm. "You look lovely."

* * *

From my bedroom window, I could see the barn as well as the lower pastures and often sat there watching the horses graze in the cool night air. When I turned off the lamp on my nightstand, the lights in the apartment over the barn were dark.

* * *

Greer made a huge production of getting ready for the riding lesson. I put on chaps over my jeans while she slithered into last year's show breeches and her brown field boots polished to a high shine. She looked like a model for the Dover Saddlery catalog.

When I went into the barn, Tracy, the local girl who was part of our crew, had Sans Egal on cross ties tacked and ready to go. I got Butch ready myself as always; he nickered to me as I approached and offered him a carrot. He took it from my hand and I ran my hand down his sleek neck, hoping for if not the best at least not the worst.

Ten minutes later, I was mounted and walking him around the outdoor ring.

Greer trotted up to me. "He's late."

I glanced at my watch. "Not by my watch."

She glanced at her blue-faced Rolex. "Wear a real watch that keeps time for change."

I wore a cheap watch in the barn, anything priced around $10 because I broke several each season.

"I'm telling Dad."

"You're going to tattle on him?" I asked.

"Report back on his newest employee," Greer corrected, giving me a look and trotted off to warm up.

That he was already on her bad side, might not be the most unfortunate thing that ever happened to him.

"Good morning, ladies," Lockie said as he walked into the ring, after closing the gate behind him.

He was wearing close-fitting black jeans, paddock boots, a blue polo shirt and sunglasses.

"You're late, don't let it happen again," Greer said. "I have things to do today."

Lockie glanced at his watch. "Right on time according to the Atomic Clock."

"It doesn't matter what the time is on the Atomic Clock, your watch is off," Greer retorted.

"By how much?" He asked.

"Three minutes," she snapped back.

"Then you can leave three minutes early."

Greer shook her head.

I thought this was starting out very well. She was already annoyed with him.

Or it was foreshadowing. I wasn't sure yet which.

"Take the rail and trot, please."

"Are we going to have a real lesson?"

"It's up to you, Miss Swope. It all depends on how much effort you want to put in on this."

"I don't have time to kill. I haven't qualified for the National yet."

The National Horse Show was the center of her life. It always had been. What happened next year when we weren't juniors any longer was not worth considering.

"I have a show in two weeks," Greer said as she trotted around the ring.

"I understand."

"I keep losing to Nicole. What makes her so great?"

"She has a very good horse and a very strong work ethic," Lockie replied. "I saw her ride last month at Devon."

The Devon Horse Show and County Fair in Pennsylvania was one of the most prestigious in the country. It was also one of the oldest horse shows in the East having begun in the late 1800s. We had attended a few times but in the past couple years Greer decided it was too far to go when she could just as easily be closer to home.

"Do I need a new horse? Because if I do, that shouldn't get in my way."

"Why don't you just concentrate on your riding for the next fifty-two minutes?" Lockie suggested.

"All I want are results," Greer replied. "Your life will be so much better if I get them."

"I'm glad we can be so forthcoming with each other this early in our relationship," Lockie said.

I thought that translated to "shut the hell up and ride"

but maybe that's just what I'd say to her if our positions had been reversed.

We worked on the flat for about fifteen minutes, trotting, cantering, changing directions, then more of the same in the opposite direction, just like at a horse show. Without commenting, he simply watched us ride. I would have preferred to be out on one of the trails through the woods. It wasn't that I disliked flat work, it was just that this was preparation for something I didn't want to do. We had a show in two weeks and if I never rode in another equitation class, it would not be one of my life's major regrets.

"Walk, please."

I pulled Butch up and we walked.

"Pick up the pace. We're not out for a morning stroll," Lockie said.

Was he talking to me?

"Miss Margolin, would you trot your horse directly to me?"

I nudged Butch into a trot and turned to go down the center of the ring.

"Thank you. Dismount. You're done for the day."

"Why?"

"Your horse is lame. Take him into the barn and call the vet so we can have some pictures taken."

Radiographs? That was serious. I threw my leg over the saddle and slid to the ground. "He doesn't feel off to me."

"He is," Lockie said.

I flipped the stirrups over the saddle. "Was he lame when we started this morning?"

"No."

"If I . . ."

"You didn't."

"Can I get some attention here?" Greer shouted across the arena.

"Call the vet, we'll deal with it," Lockie said and turned to Greer.

I pulled the reins over Butch's head, and led him from the ring.

In the barn, I put him in the wash stall, removed the saddle and bridle, then put a halter on him. I ran my hand down each leg to feel for heat and picked up each hoof to see if a rock had been lodged next to his frog. There was nothing wrong that would account for Butch being off.

After hosing his body, I ran cool water on each leg, scraped him off and left him there to dry while I called the vet from the tack room. Feeling guilty and responsible, I kept telling myself that if I couldn't tell Butch was lame, it couldn't be serious.

At ten, Greer entered the barn, in a condition I had rarely ever seen her. She was sweating, her hair was plastered against her head and her once cute little shirt was clinging to her body. Furious didn't begin to describe her mood.

"I can hardly move," Greer practically spat at Lockie.

"If you want to place above your competition, you must work harder than your competition, Miss Swope," he told her while walking toward me.

"I'm not doing that every day," she said.

"Then you will continue to pin second. It's your choice."

"No one else ever made me work that hard."

"I'm not everyone else. Your father hired me to get you to the National Horse Show and that's my job."

"Why can't I just get a better horse?"

"You can. But you won't be a better rider on a better horse."

She shrieked at him, dropped the reins into Pavel's hand and stormed out of the barn.

Lockie turned to me. "Did you call the vet?"

"He'll be here before lunch."

"Good. Is your horse comfortable in his stall?"

"Yes. I felt his legs; there was no heat. His soles didn't seem tender. I hosed him down, let him dry off and put him away. Do I need to do anything else?"

"No, you did everything you could. If you don't need me for anything for another half hour, I'll be in the apartment. Is that all right?"

"Sure. If Dr. Fortier comes, I'll call."

"Thank you but I'll be down before then."

I watched Lockie go down the aisle and turn for the stairs.

— 3 —

JUST BEFORE NOON, the vet truck drove into the yard and I went out to meet him.

"Hi, Talia. How are you?"

"I'm fine but Butch isn't."

"What's his problem?"

"We have another new trainer."

Dr. Fortier opened the back of the truck and dipped his head so I wouldn't see the grin.

"You can laugh, it won't hurt my feelings."

"How many is that this year?"

"Four."

"Okay. Who is it this time?"

"He's from California. He was pretty well known a couple years ago as a junior."

"Lockie Malone?" Dr. Fortier pulled the portable x-ray machine out and set it on the tailgate.

"That's right. He arrived yesterday and today was our first lesson. About halfway in, he said Butch was off and to call you."

"Has Butch been ouchy?"

"I haven't noticed anything."

As we went into the barn, I recounted the history of the past couple weeks. We hadn't hit any fences, we hadn't even trained very hard since Rui left, although I rode every day.

With Butch on some cross ties, Lockie turned and walked down the aisle to meet us, not wearing sunglasses any longer but regular glasses with a little tint. I thought perhaps they were the kind that were light in the dark and darker in the sunlight.

"Dr. Fortier? Hi, I'm Lockie Malone."

"Hi. I hear Talia's horse is sore."

"Something's going on."

"Okay, I'll talk your word for it and we'll check him out. Talia, remind me how old Butch is."

"I got him when we were both eleven."

"That was a big horse for a little girl."

"I was never very small. I outgrew the pony stage very early on."

"Is that why you have those two ponies now?"

"I love ponies," I admitted.

An hour later, we were looking at the X-rays he had taken.

"You can see some bone changes here and here." Dr. Fortier pointed. "And he's got some arthritis. It's normal for his age."

"There's nothing we can do, is there?"

"Make him comfortable," Dr. Fortier said. "You can give him some supplements, Bute for pain. You can hack out in the woods once in a while, but his show days are over."

"Did I do this to him?"

"Age did," Lockie replied.

"Horses only look strong and everyone starts to wear with age. It'll happen to you, too," Dr. Fortier said with a smile.

I didn't feel like smiling and went into Butch's stall while Lockie and the vet went outside.

We had been together since before my mother died. She'd been ill for a few years and it was obvious to me that she was never going to get better. She had a transparency overtaking her where each day she faded a bit more.

My father had been managing almost everything for those years as it became progressively more difficult for her to conduct her life. He made the arrangements for the hospitals and the doctors and begged her to marry him again and again until she finally gave in so that my future wouldn't be in question.

He moved us to the farm and to give me something to

try to take my heart and mind off what was happening, Butch was found for me.

Greer hated it. Blaming my mother for destroying her own family, she didn't want me in the house. That September a boarding school in Virginia became her new home; she was as happy as Greer ever is. Her mother is still happily living in London on the extremely generous divorce settlement my father offered.

I had Butch and quiet and ever-present apprehension.

Then the time came when even with full time nursing, my mother had to go to the hospital and she never came home.

My father returned to the city, a nanny was brought in for me, and a trainer. I lived alone for the rest of that school year. When Greer came back from Virginia, we started in on the serious equitation and junior hunter training.

The rug had been pulled out from under me again and I buried my face in Butch's neck and cried.

"Talia," Lockie said from behind me. "He's retiring, not dying."

"He's my best friend."

"We'll get you a new friend."

"Idiot," I said, turned and pushed past him.

* * *

We were seated around the dinner table. I would have preferred to be anywhere else but there was so much I couldn't do anything about.

"If Talia needs a new horse, get her a new horse," my father said to Lockie after the news had been relayed.

"Why should she get a new horse and I don't get a new horse? I will never beat Nicole on Sans."

I looked to Lockie who was at the far end of the table. His glasses now had a tint, enough that I couldn't really see his eyes and his face didn't show any reaction to Greer's outburst.

"Get Greer a new horse, too. Maybe we should start buying them in sets so we'll have spares."

"What am I going to ride for the show?"

"Ride your horse," I said to her.

"He's an embarrassment. Dad!"

"I'll have a couple horses sent on trial," Lockie replied.

I finished my dinner.

* * *

Under continuing loud protests, Greer rode Sans the next day for a lesson. I could have ridden one of the other horses but didn't want to and Lockie didn't mention it to me.

I met Rogers for a hamburger and a movie that I didn't understand at all but she was practically swooning over. Even though there were subtitles, I wasn't paying any attention and she felt it was necessary to explain everything to me. Luckily, the theater was nearly empty so no one complained about her whispering.

After returning home, I took a shower and sat at my window watching Butch in the field, thinking about all the times he had gotten me out of tight spots either on a trail ride or at a horse show. That kind of relationship wasn't replaceable just because there was money enough to buy a new friend. Greer didn't have a clue who she was riding and she didn't care. It was all about beating Nicole. But what would happen if she did triumph over her arch rival? What would happen if Greer won the Maclay at the National Horse Show? Then what? What happened next year? Having achieved her goal, what was left? Greer had never mentioned anything else.

As for me, I had no achievable goals.

I turned off the light and got into bed.

THE SOUND OF A TRUCK ENTERING the stable yard woke me and I went to the window but couldn't see the license plate or read the lettering on the side because of the angle. The sun wasn't up yet and the mist was rising from the pastures. Lockie, Pavel and two other men opened the door to the van and lowered the ramp. Four horses were lead into the barn.

They looked excellent from my vantage point. One appeared to be about 16.2 hands high and was dark brown. There were two bays and a chestnut, maybe a mare, smaller and more delicate than the tallest one.

Greer had a nice selection awaiting her.

I pulled on some jeans and went downstairs to the kitchen where Jules was making breakfast. "Why is everything happening so early?" I asked, sitting down at the island.

She placed a glass of mango nectar in front of me. "Big day for test driving horses," she said with a wide smile.

Jules didn't ride and had no desire to learn. She was from California, where her father was some bigshot in Hollywood and that fact had made it almost impossible for her to be her own person she said. So Jules left home and went to study cooking in Paris. Now she was with us and seemed happy all the time. I thought Jules understood the difficulties presented by having a father who had money, influence and too many demands on his plate.

"What would you like for breakfast?"

"Pancetta," I replied. I liked the Italian unsmoked bacon she had introduced to us.

"Some eggs?"

"Sure. Am I the only one eating?"

"Right now you are."

"Don't you feel like a short order cook? Whatever time of day it is, you have to start cooking."

Jules smiled. "That's my job. If I worked at a restaurant, I'd be doing that all day long and for two or three hundred people. My life is easy. All I have to do is cook for you, sometimes Greer, sometimes your father."

"And now Lockie."

"Mr. Malone. He's an interesting one, isn't he?" She placed a plate of breakfast pastries in front of me.

"What makes him interesting?"

Jules took the eggs and the package of bacon from the refrigerator. "For starters, he's not flirting with Greer."

"And she's sure not flirting with him. She's not real happy with him."

Jules was enjoying the thought of it. "He's making her work and she hasn't been able to wrap him around her little finger yet."

"He caved on the get-her-a-new-horse routine."

"Your father did. Lockie knew an order when he heard it. Your father wanted to make life easy for everyone and give her want she wanted."

"How does that make it easier?" I cut the pastry in half.

"It's only temporary."

"She's running out of time to qualify. Changing horses every two weeks won't do it for her."

"Can't Greer just ride the new one next weekend? I don't understand any of this."

I nodded. "It's better if you know the horse and the horse knows you. You build trust, a rapport. Like with a person, you begin to know them, know what to expect from them. You can anticipate their next move, making it possible to work together as a team, not as two separate individuals."

"I never realized it was so complicated. It's not for me," Jules admitted as she turned the pancetta over in the pan. "I'll leave it to you."

"I don't know why I need a new horse now."

"Don't you want to go to the big show? Isn't it like the Academy Awards? The crowning glory, what everyone exists for?" Jules placed the bacon on a paper towel and cracked two eggs into the pan.

"No, I can live without it quite easily."

"What do you want to do?"

I shrugged. "When did you know you wanted to be a chef?"

Jules' smile lit up the room. "All the women in my family are terrific cooks. They always brought me into the kitchen and let me stand on a chair so I could help. The decision wasn't that much of a choice; it was just a continuation of my childhood."

"Why don't you have your own restaurant?"

"Do you want to get rid of me?"

"God, no. If you left, I'd have no one."

"You're going to college in a year." Jules put the eggs on a plate, placed some berries alongside them, lay the strips of pancetta down and put the plate in front of me.

"Am I?"

Greer had been looking at colleges with riding programs. After winter break, that was all she talked about. Then we got a new trainer and she became more interested in Rui. He was all she talked about. He was such a terrific rider and trainer. He understood equestrian sports differently than Americans did. He was so . . . European.

I pointed out that Rui is South American which is quite a distance from Europe.

Greer had snapped back that he had spent the last five years riding in Europe and that's what gave him a unique perspective.

"Stop shining up to your boyfriend," I had told her.

Greer had screamed at me, flung her paddock boot in my general direction and went up to her room. Twenty minutes later, she had changed and drove off, spinning the tires of her Porsche Boxster on the way out of the yard.

If I was going to college, I had to make sure it was at least a thousand miles from wherever she went.

I finished breakfast and was having a conversation with Jules about food in the French countryside when Greer entered the kitchen.

"Good morning, what would you like for breakfast?"

She made a face. "Qualifying for the Maclay."

"I'm sorry, I don't have that in the refrigerator. Would you like a Danish? It's fresh."

"It's full of butter."

"Laminated," Jules replied. "Hundreds of layers of butter."

"Disgusting."

"I thought it was delicious," I replied and stood up.

"Have you seen the horses yet?" Greer asked as I walked out of the house with her."

"From my bedroom window."

"And?"

"They're beautiful. You should be happy."

"I get first choice."

"Of course you do," I said with a laugh. "You can have all of them."

The van that had brought the horses was gone and we would have a week to decide. It was the usual arrangement but Greer often made up her mind much more quickly, sometimes just by looking. Did the horse go with her hair color type of decision.

We entered the barn and there were two horses on cross ties.

"No," Greer said as she looking at the seal brown horse.

Lockie came out of the tack room.

"What is this?" Greer asked, pointing at the horse.

"A very fine ami-owner hunter from North Carolina."

"I need an equitation horse."

"You need a horse for the weekend. He has an excellent reputation."

"Let Talia ride him, she won't look like she was put in the dryer and shrunk on him. I'll ride the bay."

I was taller than Greer, something she never let me forget, and it meant I always rode the bigger horses.

"Is that okay with you, Talia?" Lockie asked.

"It doesn't matter," I replied as I went to get my saddle.

"Hello? Pavel? Do I have to do everything?" Greer asked impatiently and he hurried off to get her tack.

Ten minutes later, I had climbed up on the mounting block while Lockie stood at the horse's head and held him for me.

"Let's use the indoor arena this morning," he said as I began to walk the horse to the outside ring.

Switching direction, I guided the horse toward the indoor.

"Why?" Greer asked.

"I want us to be able to concentrate on the business at hand. Horses in the field or the hay truck arriving shouldn't be a distraction."

It made sense to me.

Inside the indoor arena, it was darker than the outside ring would have been, but there were fences and markers just the same. We rode on the flat for about twenty minutes but I couldn't get comfortable on the horse. He had a very long stride and at the trot, I felt propelled out of the saddle. The canter was as bad although in a different way. He covered a lot of ground and it was so such a change from Butch that I didn't think I'd ever get used to it or grow to like it.

The horse understood the cavelletti, rails placed on the ground to trot over, perfectly well and adjusted the length of his stride. Even still, I felt loose and out of sync with him. When Lockie set up a low fence at the end of the set, that's when the problems started.

"Talia, try to hold him together, stabilize him between the bit and your legs."

I didn't bother to answer. That was what I had been trying to do.

Greer's horse flew through the set and over the low jump with no trouble, although far too rapidly.

"Okay, this is something we can work on," Lockie said almost in resignation. "Greer, would you take the fences on the outside?"

"Any course?"

"Just twice around will be fine," he replied.

Greer made a small circle and took the four fences two times.

"Talia?"

The fences were higher than I expected, more like what we'd see at a show—two-foot-nine or three-feet. Why did we have to start there on a strange horse that I didn't even like?

I was sitting still.

Lockie was in the middle of the arena creating an oxer out of two fences. "Please go next."

I didn't move.

He stopped what he was doing and looked up.

"I get blamed for everything. I have high standards that somehow people find difficult to accept but there's the problem child," Greer said loudly as she walked her horse in a large circle at the entrance.

"Have I missed something?" Lockie asked. "Someone talk to me."

"I'm talking to you," Greer called out.

"Thank you, I would like to hear from Talia." He came over to me, standing by my knee. "I've seen this horse at shows. He's well-schooled and very good over fences, just point him."

"His stride," I started.

"He does have big stride. Hold him together. Be firm."

I shook my head as I turned the horse around, made a small circle and headed him to the first fence. He stood back so far I was nearly launched out of the saddle. Pulling the horse up, I didn't even bother considering continuing.

"Excuse me?"

"She doesn't like jumping," Greer explained to him. "Major Chickensh . . ."

"Shut up for once," I said to her and left the arena.

I slid off the horse outside the barn and brought him inside.

"Do you want me to take him, Miss Margolin?" Pavel asked.

"Yes, please," I said handing him the reins and went to Butch's stall where I opened the door, went inside and closed the door. He was eating hay and I sat down on the clean straw near him.

Nothing bothered Greer. Things that bothered most people anyway. She'd throw a fit if a store didn't have her size in the shoes she wanted, but getting attached to horses or trainers or schools or friends wasn't part of her character.

She didn't seem to miss her mother who was still very alive and could be visited.

I missed my mother every day. She would tell me I didn't need to try out these new horses and didn't have to go to horse shows or jump fences or try to win ribbons. She would have been very happy to have me at home with her.

She had been happy to have me home with her. We used to read in bed or listen to music, talking about all the places we both knew we would never visit.

This was like a nightmare. I know why she married him, it was for me, but I didn't know what she saw in him in the first place.

My father was someone I barely knew. I wasn't sure anyone knew him, although he seemed to have a great many friends. He ran his businesses mostly from the office in the city and was involved in politics that I not only couldn't understand, I didn't want to understand. There was inherited wealth but he was no slouch at making money.

If only I had cared, I would have been happier here. I could have been like Greer replacing relationships with the acquisition of things. My father indulged her, gave her everything she wanted because he couldn't give her the one thing she didn't have—a real father.

"Talia?" Lockie said quietly as he slid the stall door open. I didn't look up and he crouched down next to me.

"Are you okay?"

"Yes."

"Do you want to try the other horse?"

I turned to him and something made me pause. "How long have you been up?"

He looked at me curiously. "Since three. The driver got lost on the way and took the wrong bridge across the Hudson River."

I started to stand, he held out his hand to help me and we stood together.

"If you don't like any of these horses, I'll find you something else."

"There's no time before the show."

"I wish I still had my horse, you could ride him."

"What happened to him?"

"I sold him last year."

"You probably buy and sell a lot of horses."

"Some but he was my horse."

The chestnut mare was tacked and standing on cross ties on the aisle.

"She's too small for you. I thought she might suit Greer but just ride her around and pretend. I'll have them sent back tomorrow."

"Okay."

"Actually, I think I know someone in Rhode Island," Lockie said unclipped the tied and lead the horse outside.

"Do they even have names?" I asked as I took the steps up the mounting block.

"Sure. Chestnut horse. Bay horse. Brown horse."

I settled myself in my saddle. "She'll be a cute horse for a novice rider."

"Yes, she will."

I followed him into the arena where Greer was already warming up the bay horse and Lockie took his position in the center.

We worked on the flat for about fifteen minutes. The mare had a barrel that required much shorter legs than mine. An eleven year old would be perfect on her.

After a few passes over the cavaletti, we were ready to begin working over fences. Greer did an egg-roll course instead of just twice around the outside.

"Talia, please take the horse over some fences," Lockie requested.

She was cute but I didn't want to ride her anymore. I didn't want to jump a horse I didn't have any leg on. Her barrel fell away at my knee.

"Give up!" Greer called. "Didn't you learn your lesson earlier? She will only jump Butch."

"Thank you for the input, Greer," he replied. "Maybe today will be different."

I urged the mare forward and went to the center of the ring where I studied him for a long moment, sensing something but not quite able to define.

"Yes?"

"I want to apologize to you."

Lockie took a step closer to the horse. "It's unnecessary."

"It's very necessary," I replied. "I'm sorry I called you an idiot. It was . . ."

"You were upset."

"That's not a good excuse."

"Is it possible for you two stop yammering so we can get on with this lesson?" Greer shouted.

I sighed. This was important. "Could you take off your sunglasses so I can see who I'm talking to?"

Slowly he pulled the glasses away from his face. His eyes were red and tearing. Immediately, he began squinting against the low light entering the arena from the upper windows.

"Okay?" Lockie pushed the sunglasses back in place.

That he was in discomfort was obvious, perhaps it was even pain. The last thing he needed was to be standing in a ring getting footing particles kicked up into his eyes.

"I don't know what makes you think you can come here to my indoor, tell me what horse to ride and what jumps to take. I've had enough. Send these crappy horses back where they came from and don't bother me again until you find something decent!"

I turned the horse around and trotted out of the ring.

"You are a spoiled brat!" He called after me.

"Way to go, Talia!" Greer cheered.

When I jumped off the horse outside the arena, I saw him leave by the side door.

As I put my saddle in the tack room, Lockie passed me on his way to his apartment.

"Thank you," he said quietly and continued up the stairs.

— 5 —

I TOOK A SHOWER, changed and went down to the kitchen
for lunch.

"It's just us," Jules said.

"What do you mean?"

"Greer left to have lunch at the Cupboard with her
friends and Lockie called to say he wasn't hungry."

"That's impossible."

"Why?"

"He didn't have breakfast."

"Not with us, but maybe he had something over there."

"Would you make him a basket and I'll take it over."

"Okay. What do you think he would like?" Jules pulled
out a loaf of crusty bread she had made.

"Not that," I said quickly.

"What's wrong with this?"

"Do you have something softer? A croissant?"

"Yes. It's a strange request; everyone likes a good, crusty bread."

Unless each time you chew, it hurts like a hammer being slammed against your head.

"Will you explain it?"

"When I come back, I will. Do you have some soup?"

"I do. Knowing how much you like beets, I made you some borscht. It's nice and cold. There's sour cream to go with it."

Jules was already pulling items out of the refrigerator, and in a few minutes had a three-course lunch nestled in a small basket complete with a thermos full of soup and a red plaid napkin.

"Thanks, Jules."

"Good luck with whatever you're trying to do. Greer said you had a blow-out with him."

"It wasn't."

"A small disagreement?"

"Sorry to disappoint everyone," I replied and started across the yard.

"It seemed like it, though," Jules called after me.

I nodded.

Pavel and Tracy were bringing horses in from the fields as I entered the barn and went up the stairs to the apartment.

I tapped on the door. "Lockie? It's Tali."

"Door's open."

I entered and found him lying on the sofa, now wearing the photochromic glasses. "I brought you lunch."

"Thank you. I'll eat later."

It sounded like a struggle to say each word.

I sat down on the small table next to the sofa. "So if I'm going to be covering for you, I think I should know what I'm covering."

"It's not necessary."

"How much pain are you in?"

"How do you know if I am?"

"My mother was in pain every day for the last year of her life. I know what it looks like."

"Between us?"

"I don't know why it makes a difference."

"I need this job."

"Having a medical issue is not a fireable offense. Having sex with Greer is the only thing that will get you fired. And a couple others but they apply to every job."

Lockie paused.

"Did you take something?"

"It'll kick in soon."

"Do you want to wait until then to tell me?"

"No. Here's the short version. The longer version is just longer.

"After I got out of Juniors, I started doing Combined

Training. I was still involved in open jumpers but was more interested in eventing. After about a year, I moved to Kentucky to work with the Ruhlmanns."

"I've heard of them. They're very good."

"Very." He closed his eyes and tried to find a more comfortable position on the sofa but that had to be impossible on that old thing. "I found a young horse. I called him Wingspread and everyone could see his potential. He's big and bold, smart and kind. Just such a unique individual.

"We were doing the cross country course at an event in Virginia and it had poured overnight. The ground was a mess. Wing came up to a berm with water in front of it and he lost his footing. I'm told I was catapulted over his head and hit the bank. I don't remember that day or any day for the next month. Then for weeks I could only remember the current day. Every day was like a fresh start."

"But your family was with you."

"No one was with me except the doctors and nurses." It took a moment for him to continue. "Anyway, it doesn't matter because I finally got better."

"Where's Wingspread?"

"I sold him to the Ruhlmanns to pay for the hospital bill. It didn't nearly cover it. I'll be paying that off for the rest of my life at the rate I'm going."

"Didn't you have . . ."

"Talia, it is what it is," Lockie said over me.

"You have medical insurance now."

"Yes, your father is very generous." Lockie paused and sighed.

"The pill kicked in." I saw the change in his face.

"You're very observant."

"Yeah. So you have fierce headaches and light sensitivity. Did you break anything in this accident?"

"A couple bones. Talia, it's all manageable."

"Is there anything else you're not telling me? I bet if you went head first into a hard object, there's more."

"It's all getting better, slowly, but improving."

"When's the last time you went to a doctor?"

"March. April. Something like that."

"You need to find a doctor here."

"I've been here three days. Is it three days?"

"Yes."

"Everything will eventually be organized. Tell . . ."

He couldn't think of the name.

"Greer?"

"Yes, Greer, that she has a lesson later this afternoon."

"She booked."

"Is she coming back?"

I shrugged. "I doubt it. Consider it an afternoon off."

"You could have a lesson."

"Mr. Malone, I have things to do. See you at dinner."

* * *

Returning to the house, I went to my father's office and knocked on the door.

"Come in."

I opened the door and stepped inside the wood-paneled library he used as his office when in the country.

"Talia. This is unusual."

"Do you have a few minutes?"

"Of course." He put down his pen and closed the lid to his laptop computer. "Stocks. Nothing important."

"I have a favor to ask. A couple actually."

He was more perplexed than before. "Are you all right?"

"Yes. I would like you to buy me a horse."

"Isn't Lockie in the process of getting horses for you and Greer to try?"

"Yes, he is. This is a horse named Wingspread and he's owned by the Ruhlmanns in Orchardiana, Kentucky. I don't know what he's worth . . ."

"Just get him." My father wrote the information down on a blank piece of paper.

I nodded.

"Okay."

"Second favor. Here's something you're really good at."

"This is a day for surprises."

Just thinking about it refreshed the emotions and tears came to my eyes. "You did everything you could for my mother. I never thanked you for that but I appreciated the extra time you gave us."

"I wish I could have done more. It's difficult to rewrite history, not always impossible, but you can't change the facts. We would all like a second chance at one time or another in order to do things with the wisdom you got by making the mistakes in the first place. So many times in life you can fix what you did wrong. This I couldn't. I'm not very good at the love thing, as I demonstrate every day, but in my clumsy way I loved her and . . . you."

I took a deep breath. "I believe that. Lockie had a riding accident a year ago and you, better than anyone, can find him the right doctors. Will you do that for me?"

"Of course. I'll take care of both of those things this afternoon."

"Don't make him feel beholden to us."

"I wouldn't dream of it."

"Thank you." I stood to leave so he could get back to his stocks and whatever he shifted around all day long.

"There wasn't time for your mother to teach me how to be a husband; maybe you'll teach me how to be a father."

"Maybe," I said at the doorway and left.

— 6 —

"Is he really cute?"

Rogers was sitting on my bed as I dressed. Still not having seen Lockie, she had come over, inviting herself for dinner as she often did. No one blamed her because her parents were *in absentia* most of the time. Then we were going to another movie she had to see. It was something in French from fifty years ago and I couldn't have cared less but getting away for a couple hours seemed like a good idea.

"Is he," she repeated.

"Yes, he's attractive."

"Like a male model handsome?"

"He's a normal person. Don't start drooling and lay your head on his boot or something during dinner."

"What's the deal with Greer?"

"She's not hanging over him. Since she skipped her lesson this afternoon, she can't be that interested."

"She'll never qualify," Rogers replied.

No, Greer wasn't going to qualify and there was nothing Lockie could do about it. It was something she felt entitled to and that didn't require effort.

That wasn't how the world worked and my mother had made me understand that from the earliest time. Nothing was made easy for me. My mother helped, but I had to do the majority of the work and the older I got, the more work I had to do on my own.

It was never expected that I was going to qualify because Butch wasn't as good of an equitation horse as Nicole's and I would never place above Greer. If Greer didn't show, I didn't go. During most of the spring Sans Egal was lame, so I had weeks of peace.

Rui thought Sans would come back sooner than he did and there was no point in starting on a new horse. That was partially right except Rui didn't appreciate the deadline Greer was facing. He wasn't from America and maybe it was just another horse show to him.

It would have been smarter to get a backup horse over the winter but no one thought of that, Greer least of all, since skiing and ski instructors had distracted her.

At home, while she was on the slopes in Vermont, Sans waited in the barn for her. Greer had done very well with him all last year. There was no reason to think this season would be any different.

Then, in March, Nicole rode into the ring on the push-button dreamboat, Taggart, and Greer found herself in an extreme predicament. The combination of Nicole who was about as perfect an equitation rider as anyone had seen in twenty years and the perfect horse made the team unbeatable. He was the perfect junior hunter, too. Greer didn't have a hope against them so for four months she had been in a foul mood. She was supposed to win. Didn't Nicole understand?

"Is he any good as a trainer?" Rogers asked as we left my room.

"We don't even have horses."

"None of the ones he sent for were any good?"

"Rogers. They're fine, they're just not a good match here. He's very patient, he's . . ."

"What? Hot?"

"No!"

"He's not hot at all?" Rogers was disappointed.

"I'm not getting into this with you. He thinks. Lockie's intuitive and intellectual about riding. It's not so straight-forward with him."

Rogers stopped and looked at me. "I don't know what the hell you're saying."

"Greer doesn't get it either."

We went down to the kitchen and helped Jules put the finishing touches on dinner. She was starting to move utensils, napkins and glasses to the large table on the terrace. Luckily, it was east facing so the sun wasn't in our eyes at this time of day.

I was coming out with a basket of fresh rolls when Rogers gave me a poke in the ribs. "That's him," she whispered.

Looking up, I saw Lockie walking along the driveway. "I know." I whispered back and returned to the house for the salad.

A moment later Lockie was at the doorway, holding the basket with the thermos and plaid napkin. "Thank you for lunch, Jules. It was delicious." He gave me a smile. "It's so unfortunate I won't be here long to enjoy your cooking."

"You're welcome to come back any time for dinner once you leave," Jules joked.

"That's good to know," he said.

"Go out on the terrace," Jules suggested. "Find your places."

"Do we have place cards?" I asked.

"Do you need one?" Lockie asked.

"As far away from you as I can get."

"I guess I haven't made a good impression on you."

"No. You haven't even apologized from this morning."

"I'm sorry I called you a brat when you were acting like a brat," Lockie said. "Where's Greer?"

"Out with her friends," I replied going to the table.

I didn't realize how close to the surface my feelings about the last year of my mother's life were. Even though it was six years ago, the experience was fresh and raw and painful and I felt the relief now for Lockie that I would have felt for her when her pain abated for a few hours. If he felt good enough to tease me, he was pain-free for a little while.

I wondered what kind of progress my father had made on acquiring his medical history. Some clues must have been in the paperwork Lockie filled out in order to work here. My father was a smart and resourceful man; with one critical piece of information, he could learn everything given enough time.

The three of us sat at the table.

"Lockie, this is my friend and classmate Rogers Kerr."

She blushed.

"Hi, Rogers. Do you ride, too?"

She was making herself as small as she could in the chair. "Yes." The reply was barely above a whisper.

"You'll have to join us for a lesson some day."

"Really?"

"Certainly. If I'm still here."

"Maybe you'll last," I said, "if you can keep all your body parts where they belong."

Quickly, he looked down, then looked back at me. "If any of my parts strays, can I depend on you to give me a heads up?"

"If I give you anything, it won't be a heads up," I replied.

My father exited from the house, moving rapidly as usual and sat down at the head of the table. He glanced at me and gave me a little nod.

"Rogers. It's good to see you. Lockie. How are you?"

"Fine, sir."

I saw a look pass over my father's face. It was doubt. And gone just as I recognized it.

"I made some calls this afternoon," Lockie began. "Greer is a very accomplished rider."

"Yes, she is, but both of my daughters are," my father said.

"That's true. Our immediate crisis is the issue of Greer qualifying. It's not going to happen."

"She can still ride; she has a horse. It's not like Talia's situation."

"The problem is two-fold. She doesn't practice and the horse isn't good enough to make up for what she lacks. Greer won't place over Nicole Boisvert; that's the reality."

"I'll talk to her."

"She ran herself out of time," Lockie replied. "If you want me to keep trying, I will. That's my job or if you want to get someone else, I understand."

I glanced at my father and he looked back at me.

"No, you're staying," my father said. "You signed a contract. You're stuck."

"I would hardly call it stuck," Lockie replied. "And I

think I have a solution. It doesn't help in the short-term, Greer will not make it to the Kentucky Horse Park for the Maclay, or Harrisburg for the Medal. But she can do Florida and kick start next year."

"How?"

"She's fearless. I sent for a couple ami-owner jumpers for her to try out. If we get her one that's made and one that's in training, maybe we can keep her attention focused. Greer gets easily bored."

"Boy, did you figure her out fast," I said under my breath.

Lockie smiled at me.

"When are these horses arriving?

"They should be here tomorrow, sir."

"Then we will have many new residents," my father replied and did something he had never done to me before. He winked.

— 7 —

ROGERS COULDN'T TALK ABOUT ANYTHING but Lockie on the way to the Thaden Theater. She wanted to take a lesson with him. Would that really be okay? I didn't care and didn't see why Greer would. What horse could Rogers ride? The barn was full of horses. Choose whatever size and color fit. She felt sort of paralyzed in his presence. Did I feel the same way? No. How was I able to speak to him? The same way I spoke to everyone else, by opening my mouth and forming sounds.

There was no line at the theater; there never was.

"What's this movie about?" I asked as we stood at the counter to get her Junior Mints, lemonade and popcorn.

"The wife and mistress of an abusive headmaster plot to kill him," Rogers replied.

"Not a comedy, then."

"No! They drug him, then drown him."

"Can you say overkill?"

"Then he goes missing!"

"If you know everything about this movie, why are we here?"

I could have taken Butch on a trail ride. It was cool now that the sun had set; we could have gone down to the stream where standing in the water might have made his legs feel better.

"It's a great classic! Besides, you can't stay home all the time. When's Josh coming back?"

Josh, the wannabe actor and boy friend, was doing summer stock because of the drama teacher's connections with someone putting together a tour. At school, you expect nothing so Josh was the best actor we had. Alongside people who had more experience, I suspected he would not fare well by comparison. But it was what he wanted to do, so everyone said break a leg and off he went the day after the semester ended.

He called when and if he had the chance. I was more likely to get a text message telling me "In Dubuque, m gr8."

"Soon. His parents' anniversary is coming up and last I heard he's doing *The Mousetrap* at The Olde Barn Playhouse."

It wouldn't be an exaggeration to say I had never seen a play I enjoyed. The idea of sitting still for two hours with people in the distance, speaking in voices so they could be heard in the balcony didn't appeal to me. That I would have to attend Josh's performance and then pretend to be enthusiastic could be deleted from my to-do list without being missed.

Rogers picked up her a large container of old popcorn—they didn't pop it fresh, I saw that it came in enormous plastic bags-with two pumps of fake butter on it and helped her with the rest. We walked into the theater and found seats in the exact center where Rogers preferred.

There were two trailers for the Hitchcock extravaganza scheduled next then the French film started. By the second talk-fest scene, I was asleep and didn't wake up until the houselights came on and Rogers was poking me saying it was time to go home.

When she left me off at the house, the lights in the apartment were off.

I wondered how much it took out of Lockie to smile and hold up his end of all the conversations throughout dinner. It had to be exhausting.

* * *

The next morning, I was up early and had Butch on the aisle, pulling his mane while the stalls were being mucked. I wanted him to remain as handsome as he always was, with his whiskers and fetlocks trimmed. "Retirement doesn't mean we let ourselves go," I told him from my stand on the overturned bucket.

Lockie came up from behind us and put his hand on Butch's neck. "You would make a good groom. How are you at braiding a tail?"

"Perfect," I said truthfully.

"I don't doubt that for a minute."

"Did you have breakfast?"

"Yes. Jules made me a mushroom and cheese omelet and . . . bread."

"That was brioche," I supplied.

"Yes." He laughed. "Is this how you always eat?"

"She's a first class chef, I told you that."

"Jules is like a member of your family, isn't she?"

"She is."

"Is she spoken for?"

"Are you interested in her?"

"No, just curious."

"She was seeing someone for a while and he got a job at an all-organic restaurant in Westchester County."

"That's not far from here."

I wrapped a few strands of mane around the comb and yanked. "If that's all it took to end the relationship then it couldn't have been very serious, could it?"

"I would say not." Lockie stood still for a moment. "I hear a van, maybe your next test drives have arrived."

"Maybe."

Stepping off the bucket, I followed him outside. Lockie recognized the maroon and white van immediately. Then it stopped in front of the barn. The Ruhlmann's Golden Ratio Farm Orchardiana, KY was lettered on the side.

The driver got out of the truck and came around to our side.

"Hi, Lockie, how're ya doin'?"

"I'm doing very well. Why are you here?"

"I was told to bring you a horse, so I did." The short, middle-aged man opened the door, pulled out the ramp and went inside.

A moment later, he led a mahogany bay gelding down the ramp, and handed Lockie the lead rope.

"I don't understand."

I didn't think Lockie could have been more confused.

"I'm just the stable help. Pat told me to drive him up here and we left last night."

Wingspread was a stunning horse, standing close to seventeen hands with a glistening dark red-brown coat and a head as classically beautiful as I had ever seen. He was lean and elegant, just like his trainer.

"Do you want breakfast?" Lockie asked. "A shower? A nap?"

"I ate on the road and have to be back, since we have a show to get to. Good luck with Wing, he always liked you best."

"Thank you," I said to the driver. "If you could stop at the house, it would be good for you to have a word with my father."

"Sure thing."

I knew my father would have an envelope for him.

"Glad to see you again, Lock, but stay up north. You know you're too good to compete against us."

"You're the consummate BS-er, as always," Lockie replied with a smile as the man closed up the van, went around the front and got inside.

Lockie looked to me. "Talia? Is there an explanation?"

"You said he'd be perfect for me."

He held out the lead rope to me but I didn't move.

"You made such a big deal about how wonderful he is but now that I see him in person, he doesn't appeal to me at all. You keep him," I said and turned back to the barn.

"Tali?"

"You need a horse, don't you?" I didn't look back. I couldn't trust myself.

Butch's stall was done so I unclipped him and led him back inside. There was fresh water and hay. He would be fine for hours.

There was the sound of metal shoes on the aisle then they stopped.

I gave Butch's nose a kiss and turned.

"I want to talk to you."

"If it's anything important, my morning's full. Maybe

later this afternoon or tomorrow." I went out onto the aisle and closed the stall door.

"What else did you do?"

"I didn't do anything and that's the truth."

"What did you set in motion?"

I shrugged.

"Is Butch sound?"

"He seems fine."

"Let's hack to the stream and let them stand in the water for a while. Wing's legs are a little stocked up from all the hours in the van. Then you can tell me what you didn't do."

"Okay."

Twenty minutes later, we were in the stream that ran through the woods, with the horses knee deep in running water. I leaned forward and lay down on Butch's neck, closing my eyes. It felt so peaceful.

"Talia, tell me what else you did."

I lifted my head and turned so I was facing him then lay back down on Butch's neck.

"He's like your pet pony," Lockie said.

I smiled. "I love how he smells, so clean and fresh. His coat is soft and I feel close to him out here."

"You can ride Wing until we find you a horse. He's still perfect for you."

"No."

"Why not? Butch isn't the only horse for you."

"Wing is perfect for you."

"How do you know?"

"Your energy is the same. You're even built alike."

"I'm not going to be riding much."

"Maybe that will change."

"Is that what you did?"

"My father did. He found you a specialist. You'll go, you'll be taken care of. Let my father do what he's really good at."

"I don't . . ."

"It's not for you, it's for me."

"How is it for you?"

I sat up and steered Butch for home. "I can't stand to see anyone in pain."

8

GREER WAS IN HER NORMAL MOOD when we reached the barn.

"Is that my new horse?" She asked eyeing Wingspread covetously.

"That's Lockie's horse," I replied throwing my right leg over Butch's neck and sliding down to the ground.

"I need a horse," Greer said all but stamping her feet and demanding Cocoa Puffs.

"There are four horses coming momentarily for you both to try out," Lockie said as he dismounted.

"This one is a good one, why can't I ride it?"

"Because it's an event horse and you don't do combined training," I replied leading Butch past her. "You need an equitation horse or . . ."

"Greer, I want to talk to you about your immediate future," Lockie began.

"Well?"

Like you don't have one, I thought bringing Butch into the wash stall. He would have been sweating under the saddle pad and a quick rinse would make him more comfortable.

"You're not going to qualify," Lockie said.

I wasn't sure if Greer said anything or if she was just screaming.

"You don't take this process seriously," Lockie said into the wailing.

"I need a better horse!"

"You need to work. You missed your lesson yesterday, and it's almost noon and you're just now dragging yourself out of bed. I'm sure Nicole has already put in two hours on her horses and will put in another two once it cools off."

"You are so fired," Greer shouted at him.

I stepped out of the wash stall to confront her. "Run that by Dad and see how it flies."

Greer shrieked at me, rushed out of the barn and headed toward the house.

"That went well," Lockie said calmly.

"Do you feel okay?" I took the hose off the wall.

"Yes, what can I do for you?"

"Nothing. I just didn't want Greer's temper tantrum to give you a headache."

"No, she didn't."

I laughed. "Aren't you lucky? She gave me one." I sprayed the water on Butch's back and between his legs, then hung up the hose. The excess water was removed from his coat by the sweat scrapper, and I was ready to put him away.

"Tali," Lockie started.

"Yes?" I unclipped the cross ties.

"Wing really doesn't appeal to you?"

I led Butch to his stall. "Be serious, Lockie. He's gorgeous."

"Will you do twenty minutes on him this afternoon?"

"If that's what you want." I gave Butch a pat and closed the door.

"I'm just thinking," he said.

"How about if we just eat?"

He wasn't following my change of topic.

"Lunch?"

He glanced at his watch. "I'm not . . ."

"Yes, you are."

"Okay, okay. Give me fifteen minutes to take care of Wing and I'll meet you up at the house."

Greer was still screaming by the time I got there. She dogged my father into the kitchen where Jules was making lunch.

"I thought he was hired to get me to Lexington," Greer complained.

I washed my hands at the sink, then splashed water on

my face. "Did you expect him to do it for you? He made it to the National on his own. You should have been able to make it on your own," I said as Jules handed me a kitchen towel to use to dry off.

"What do you know about it?"

"I know you have to work for what you want."

"I work! If I had a decent horse . . ."

Opening the door, Lockie stepped inside. "Oops. Bad timing."

"Who stayed sound for more than two weeks in a row, maybe things would be a little bit better. Don't you think?" Greer glared at me.

"If you spent more time on the horse and less time on Rui, maybe that would have been a little bit better," I replied.

"Enough," my father said. "We're not doing this."

"I need a new trainer. Someone with a positive attitude." Greer glared at Lockie.

"If you want to find yourself a new trainer, that's fine. You can get yourself a horse and keep it at that barn and drive yourself over there every day but Lockie is going to be training the horses here," my father told her evenly. "Where are we eating?"

"Since the weather is so lovely, on the terrace," Jules replied.

"That'll be nice," my father said as he went outside with Lockie.

Greer followed him.

"She's like a banshee," I said softly.

Jules did everything she could not to burst into laughter.

"How am I going to have a life and board a horse some-place else?"

"I don't know."

"Who am I going to ride with this far into the season? I mean Tick-Tock. Tempus Fugit."

That's a good name for a horse, I thought as I stood in the doorway.

"Greer, you're old enough to figure these things out for yourself," my father said.

I was very impressed. He usually gave in immediately to shut her up.

She shrieked.

Birds flew out of the trees in fright.

Jules gave me a push to leave the kitchen. The terrace was the last place I wanted to be with Greer doing a star turn.

She did this to herself. Greer had made no serious con-tribution to qualifying this year. Between visiting friends in Millbrook and having the whatever it was with Rui, there was hardly fifteen minutes left over for riding.

Rui may have been short-listed for the Brazilian team but he was an incompetent instructor. With his thick accent, minimal understanding of English and spending an inordinate amount of time studying Greer's position in her skin-tight breeches, it was a lark to him as well.

With no ego-gratification to be gained from showing, the less attention Rui paid to my "position" the better I liked it.

Lockie came over and sat next to me at the foot of the table.

"So your horse arrived in one piece?" My father asked as he started in on the salad.

"Yes, sir, thank you. I don't know how to pay you back, either of you."

"What? Is there something going on I don't know about?" Greer asked.

"Life at the farm," I replied.

"If we wind up with some fine horses, and Bittersweet Farms is mentioned in the papers once in a while, that's plenty."

"Dad," Greer objected. "That's nothing."

"That's the future. There's no more equitation. There's no more junior competitions. You're both adults now."

"I'm not an adult yet," Greer protested.

"If you act like one, as you proved by your conduct with Rui, then you are one," my father replied.

Greer pushed back from the table and strode into the house.

We all sighed in relief.

* * *

"What do you know about dressage?" Lockie asked as he gave me a leg up onto Wing.

"Nothing."

Lockie didn't reply.

"No, in all the years I've been taking lessons, not one teacher ever mentioned the word dressage until just now."

"It's okay. I'm a product of the same system. Equitation is the main focus here, but I was lucky early on and met someone from England who gave me another perspective."

He walked alongside us into the indoor arena where it was a little cooler and much shadier.

"We're going to transition you from thinking equitation to thinking dressage."

"They're such different disciplines."

"Yes. In equitation, the point is to demonstrate how pretty the rider is. In dressage, you're showing a working team."

I walked Wing around the outside of the ring while Lockie talked about dressage. He asked me to adjust my position, my hands, my back, my seat. We trotted briefly then he discussed that. He asked for a circle at a sitting trot. I had to remember to call it a collected trot.

After going both directions, he asked me to halt and explained why I didn't do it very well and how to halt correctly.

In a way, I felt as though I had never had a riding lesson until that afternoon. Nothing had ever been analyzed before. All the trainers had ever done was to stand in the middle of the ring and tell me what to do. Walk, trot, canter. Head up, heels down, back straight. Year after year, it was the same thing until I was as picture perfect as I could be and was bored out of my head.

This was the first day I felt engaged. Finally, there was a hint of logic and order to riding.

"That's enough," Lockie said after about twenty minutes.

"Is it?"

"That really is about all you or the horse can deal with."

"Then why are lessons an hour?"

Lockie laughed. "Because people charge by the hour."

I dismounted.

"This is a good start. How did it feel to you?"

"I liked it."

"I thought you might." He ran up my stirrup iron on the far side. "Do you like Wing?"

I paused.

"Say no, Tali, if you mean no."

"I like him personally."

"But he doesn't feel right to you."

"No."

"Okay. In what way, so I can find you a horse you'll feel comfortable on."

We walked out of the arena.

"I'm used to Butch."

"So you want a horse that feels big under you not just tall."

"Yes."

"You don't like the shape of a Thoroughbred."

"No. They're not round enough."

"Thank you. I know exactly what to look for. Now tell me about this you don't want to jump another horse but Butch."

I wasn't sure I could put it into words then looped the reins around my arm. "The difference between ba-dum ba-dum ba-dum," I motion with my hand as if a horse was steadily approaching a fence. "And zoom."

"At some point you rode a horse that rushed a fence and it scared the daylights out of you."

"There was a reason to be scared. He hit the standards, everything came down, and I practically fell under him."

Lockie nodded. "Good reason."

We entered the barn and stopped at the cross ties where Wingspread's halter had been left hanging.

"I'm not here to make your life miserable. I'm not here to make you unhappy. You don't ever have to jump another fence as far as I'm concerned."

"My father wants us to compete. He's always pushed us and I always felt I was failing because Greer is so super-competitive."

Lockie undid the girth and pulled the saddle off. "That part of your life is over. You're not riding in equitation classes anymore. You don't have to ride in hunter classes. You won't ever compete against Greer again."

"But my father . . ."

"When he said you're both adults now, he meant that. So if you want to ride, you ride. If you want me to find you a horse, I'll find you a horse. If you don't want a horse, I'm here to train for the barn. That's what your father wants."

"And to get Greer to shut up."

"Greer has the ideal personality for the jumper division—no fear. I just need to find someone who will ride the horse when she's off getting a pedicure. Then the day of the show, she'll get on, and the horse will drag her over the fences. Maybe she'll even win."

I looked at him.

"If I'm really lucky and find the right horse for her."

9

LATER THAT AFTERNOON, five horses arrived from Virginia. None of them were right for me but Greer's main squeeze and his backup were among the choices. She was ecstatic.

We almost were because whether she was happy or not, either way, Greer still didn't shut up.

* * *

Lockie looked worn out the next day after working with Greer in the morning as well as Tracy, who he thought could help exercise the horses, so I told him I had to go shopping for a dress for a party.

"That's fine, we're going to Pennsylvania tomorrow."

"Why?"

"There are a couple horses for you to try out."

"Why can't they come to us?"

He looked at me for a moment. "Because I would like to spend a couple hours with you off the property."

"What?"

"Yes."

"You want to drive in a truck with me for twelve hours there and back?"

"We're flying."

"We're flying?"

"Tali. There's an echo in here," Lockie said with a small smile. "We're taking a private plane. That's how it's done."

"What?"

"I can't spend that kind of time in the truck. And I have to go to New York the next day."

"Why?"

"For the doctor's appointment that you insisted upon. I'm going down to the city with your father so he told me to get the Pennsylvania trip over with as quickly as possible. It'll take an hour to fly, and we'll be there a couple hours and fly back. Done. Okay?"

The way he said it made me know something was wrong. "Yes. I'm sorry."

"About?"

"You have a headache."

"I'm sorry I snapped at you. Yes, I do."

"Go upstairs and lay down for a while. I'll take care of everything here."

He started for the stairs to his apartment.

"I'm not in a rush to get a horse. We can put it off until later, next week, whenever you're feeling better."

"The appointment is for tomorrow."

"Gotcha. I'll be ready."

* * *

That evening I got a text message from Josh saying he would be home for his parents' wedding anniversary.

This was always a large celebration on their expansive back lawn practically big enough to be a golf course. There was catered food, an open bar, multiple tents and a dance band. The finale was a fireworks display, something I always enjoyed.

Everyone in the house went. That meant Lockie would be joining us this year if he so chose.

I wasn't sure how I felt about it.

* * *

The next morning Lockie was already finishing breakfast when I entered the kitchen. Jules opened the oven door, removed a plate of food that had been being kept warm and placed it in front of me.

"Are we in that much of a hurry?" I asked, picking up a fork. "The plane's not leaving without us."

"It's seven. We have to drive to the airport."

"Which one are we going to?"

"Oxford."

"That's close."

"Eat, don't talk."

"Lockie, it'll take a half hour to drive there."

"It'll take an hour. Will you drive?"

"Of course."

"That's good because I have everything packed in your truck."

"And I made lunch for you." Jules placed a cooler by the door. "I don't know where you're going and if they have food there."

"There's food everywhere," I said.

"Please eat."

Squirting the golden syrup over the bread, I concentrated on finishing the French toast and pancetta.

Lockie was correct; it took us nearly an hour to get there even though half of the trip was on the highway. I was never very good at judging such things.

I drove into the airport parking lot and found a place, stopped and locked the truck while Lockie took my saddle from the back. "Do you feel alright?"

"The meds should kick in any time now; it usually takes about an hour."

"Did you bring some with you?"

"Yes. Don't focus on it; it's better if you don't."

"I'm glad you're going to the doctor tomorrow."

"You're just glad to have a day off."

"That's not true. Do you want me to go with you?"

"Why would you do that?"

We entered the very small terminal building.

"Because you were alone the last time."

"This will be an exam, an MRI or some scan, and I'll be back in the car headed home before noon."

"Will you call me?"

"You won't notice I'm gone."

Lockie stepped up to the counter. "We're here to meet Don Wheeler. Do you know where he is?"

"You'll find him out with his plane doing a pre-flight check." The man behind the counter pointed to a row of small aircraft. "It's the white one with the red stripes on the tail section."

"Thank you."

We went out the back door and walked to the plane.

"Hi. Mr. Wheeler?"

"Call me Don. My mother did. I won't tell you what my father called me."

Lockie held out his hand.

"You must be the people trying to get to Pennsylvania today."

"That's us," I replied. "I'm Talia Margolin."

"It's very nice to meet you. Do you get airsick?"

"No."

"That's good because it's difficult to put your head out the window at five thousand feet if you do."

"Talia's tougher than the two of us put together, she'll be fine," Lockie replied.

"That's my kind of girl," Don said with a grin. "Let's take that . . . what is it?" He asked as he opened a small storage compartment in the rear of the plane.

"It's a saddle. We're looking at horses today," Lockie said.

"That's right. Mr. Swope mentioned that when he called me. Okay, everyone get in and let's roll."

"Have you flown my father somewhere?" I asked trying not to sound too hopeful but wanting some confirmation that the man was a reasonably expert pilot.

"Yes, I have. I flew him to Canada a few months ago."

Lockie waited by the wing for me where there was a tread so passengers could step up to the small door.

"I remember that trip," I replied.

"Front seat or rear," Lockie asked.

"What's better for you?"

"It doesn't matter. You take the back going down, and the front coming home."

We climbed into the plane, which wasn't much larger inside than my truck, pulled our seatbelts tight and a few minutes later we were rising into the sky over Connecticut. Flying west, we passed over the wide expanse of the Hudson River then turned south for Pennsylvania. The Statue of Liberty was off our left wing as we flew over New Jersey.

— 10 —

TOO LOUD IN THE PLANE to talk amongst ourselves, I contented myself with looking out the window. We were skirting around huge white clouds, the sun shining bright. Of course, Lockie had on his darkest sunglasses.

The plane dropped suddenly.

"Sorry. We hit a pothole," Don said with a laugh.

"What makes that happen?" I asked

"It's just air currents. Since the sun's out, it's warm and we all know heat rises. When you fly into an area where the temperature is changing, there's some instability. The flight would be smoother in the evening, after the sun goes down."

"Thank you for the explanation."

I wondered if this trip would be a waste; it seemed like

such a big effort just to get me a horse when there wasn't a deadline. There was always a horse to ride in the barn and now that Wingspread was where he belonged, I was sure Lockie wouldn't object to letting me ride him once in a while. My hope was that Greer would be satisfied with the amateur owner jumpers she had gotten this week. I hoped the newness of Counterpoint would keep her in the saddle long enough to develop a relationship with him. Then if she decided to go shopping to visiting friends day after day, Greer might have the ability to do well at a couple shows.

A Greer with a blue ribbon was a much better experience than a Greer with a red. Not that they mattered to her, the moment she pulled the ribbon off the bridle and hung it on the trailer, the thrill was gone.

I thought more than anything she had wanted our father to take notice of her in some way that he didn't. He was always pleased and proud when either of us did well but somehow it wasn't enough for Greer. There was an empty spot in her that wasn't being filled.

Of course, her mother was as shallow as any person I had ever met. More so than my father, Victoria, busy with her friends and activities, rarely had time for Greer.

It was understandable why my father had been so enamored, in his own way, of my mother who was the complete opposite of Victoria. The truth was that no one would miss Victoria when she was gone and everyone who knew my mother still missed her six years after she passed.

Greer could have enjoyed a closeness with my mother but she could never forgive her. Someone had to be held accountable for the dissolution of the marriage, even if it had been so predictable.

Opening my tote bag, I pulled out a bottle of water, tapped Lockie on the shoulder and held it out to him. I took one for myself, uncapped it and drank. My mother always told me to stay hydrated. I tried to do everything she had told me to do. I just wished I remembered everything.

After about an hour, Don pointed out the windshield. "There's the airport."

It was smaller than Oxford as there was only one runway and no tower to direct traffic. We headed straight at it and Don expertly landed the plane, then we taxied to visitor parking.

Someone from the stable was waiting to pick us up and we, including Don, got in the SUV to be driven to the farm about fifteen minutes away.

It was a region of beautiful, rolling farmland, with white plank fences and large white houses. There were horses and dairy cows in the fields and I imagined that Connecticut had looked like this at one time.

The young woman turned the car up the long driveway to the farm and I could see there were horses still out in pastures on each side. She stopped in front of a large barn, easily twice the size of ours, and we all got out.

"Hi, Lockie," a short, thin woman with close-cropped

hair exited from the barn in a rush, and put her arms around him. "You're as handsome as ever. Married yet?"

"Not yet."

"You let me know if you want to settle down and I'll kick Faber to the curb and we can run off together."

She looked old enough to be his mother so I knew she wasn't serious. But maybe she was. He was pretty cute.

"Talia, this is Marilyn Theissen."

She took my hand and gave it a firm shake. "Glad to meet you. Lockie says you need a horse."

"That's what I'm told," I replied.

"Based on what he said, I think I might have a few of interest for you. The two youngest were born here. Three others Faber found in Germany and we shipped over."

Lockie adjusted his sunglasses and turned his back to the sun. "Is Faber there now?"

"No, he's in Maryland today giving a two-day dressage clinic and is very sorry he missed you."

"I'm sure we'll catch up with each other at some point."

"God, you look good!" Marilyn said and gave Lockie another squeeze. "I'm glad to see you."

"I'm glad to see you, too."

"Yeah." Marilyn started walking to the barn. "Let's play the Love Game and see if we can't find a match here."

Lockie turned and smiled at me. I didn't feel reassured and still didn't really want another horse. All my best riding memories had been created with Butch.

The young woman who had picked us up was in the process of putting horses on cross ties on the aisle.

"Here, let me take that from you," Marilyn said and pointed to the saddle Lockie was carrying. "Petra!"

Another young woman with light blonde hair appeared and hurried over to get my saddle.

"This is a four year old, he's just getting into training so it'll be a few years before you can compete on him. I don't know how much you know about these warmbloods," Marilyn said to me. "They're more laid-back than Thoroughbreds and get into training later. Lockie said you have been doing the hunter seat thing. It's a good place to start; I don't have a problem with it. A little limiting is all," Marilyn said, speaking rapidly. "You probably want something with a bit more mileage but he's got all the potential in the world. This is a six year old and much farther along. Spend the winter on him and next season he'll be ready to get down to business."

We followed her down the aisle and she stopped at a grey horse. "This is a Hanoverian Faber picked up in Germany this spring. He's eight and very impressive. I think we should keep him."

"You think that about every horse," Lockie pointed out to her.

"I do!"

"This bay mare, Karneval, is nine and is perfection. The drawback for her is that she doesn't have a lot of speed across country."

"I don't think we're too concerned about that," Lockie said.

"She's a nice horse if that's not a consideration. Down at the end of the aisle we have that chestnut. Good speed, good agility. In a year or two, he can be at international level."

No. That was too much for me. It felt like pressure.

"How about we start with the mare," Marilyn said.

"How about the grey horse?" I asked.

"Really? Okay. Petra, would you tack him up for us?"

"What's his name," I asked.

"Freudigen Geist. Joyful Spirit. I'd rename him to something people can remember, but that's his papered name and Faber didn't see any point in renaming him since he wasn't staying."

Petra quickly tacked the horse and led him outside.

"You want me to ride him? You want to ride him?" Marilyn asked Lockie.

"Yes, I will. Do you have a helmet I can borrow?"

"Sure. Dori, get Faber's practice helmet please."

A moment later, a young woman appeared with a helmet and held it out to Lockie.

He put it on. "It fits."

A moment later, he was on the horse and adjusting the length of my stirrup leathers. We went into their indoor arena, also about twice the size of ours, and Lockie spent the next few minutes warming the horse up. Then he began what appeared to me to be a dressage test. At the markers positioned on the wall, Lockie would transition from a walk to a sitting trot, a canter, he circled, did moves I had never seen before and definitely did not know the names of, and finished with an extended trot that was so wonderful I nearly gasped.

"Lockie is such a beautiful rider," Marilyn said softly to me. "But you know that."

Of course, I didn't know that. I'd never seen him ride except to the stream and back.

"Do you want me to lower the fences for you?"

"No, I'll just pop over that vertical a couple times to see what he's like."

After a few times going back and forth over the rails, Lockie pointed the horse at a plain fence followed by an oxer, a panel, an in and out. Some were just plain rails but they were all well above anything I ever jumped, most of them looked to be four feet.

He pulled up in front of us and dismounted.

"I'm going to go sit over there and you can talk about me behind my back, okay?"

"Okay," Lockie said with a smile as Marilyn walked away. "This is a really big horse, Talia."

"I can see that."

"Do you want to ride him?"

"Yes."

"Do you want to ride him on a lunge line first?"

"Is he going to run off with me?"

"No. You're going to need spurs with this guy."

"Really?"

"Really. But he's strong, you'll need to use your back and your seat or he won't even know you're there."

"Okay."

"Put your helmet on."

I pulled it out of my tote bag and put it on.

"I'll give you a leg up. On three."

I took the reins and Lockie boosted me into the saddle, then began helping shorten the leathers.

"Relax, he's a nice horse. You're safe on him."

I urged the horse forward and we walked around the outside track.

"Let's do a collected trot. Don't worry about keeping your legs steady, keep your legs on him."

What did that mean?

"Tempo." Lockie snapped his fingers several times to demonstrate. "Push him forward. Use your seat."

What did that mean?

I went around the ring once, then at a working trot, then we walked and cantered. Meanwhile, Lockie was lowering the plain fences to something more my speed, in the 2'6" zone.

"Come to the center of the ring."

I turned the horse and headed for Lockie.

"Are you okay?"

"Yes."

"Do you feel comfortable?"

"Yes."

"Do you want to try to jump him? No's as good an answer as yes."

"Yes," I replied.

"Good. He's a little bit sleepy but once you get him cranked up, he'll be fine."

"He's not a Thoroughbred."

"That's the difference between a Thoroughbred and a warmblood. They have a different temperament."

"I feel like I'm sitting on a skyscraper."

"He's a big horse."

"But comfortable."

"Like riding a sofa."

"Lockie," I protested.

"However you want do it, go jump him over those plain rails."

"You want me to trot or canter or what?"

"I want you to do it the way you want to."

With a shrug, I turned the horse, then urged him into a trot and headed for the fence. Working hard at it, I got him to canter and he easily cleared the fence. We kept going to the next, then the next until we had gone twice around.

Pulling him back to a walk, I returned to the center of the arena.

Looking up at me, Lockie put his hand on my knee. "So, Tali, did I find you a horse?"

I couldn't speak. That whole thing about opening my mouth and forming words wasn't working. Instead, I held out my hand to him and he took it.

— 11 —

SLEEP ELUDED ME like a fox taunts a pack of young hounds.

I had no good memory of hospitals or doctors. It began when I was nine. I knew something was wrong. My mother smiled and said everything would be all right. For the next two years, that's what I heard from everyone and had long stopped believing it.

My father did everything for her medically possible. He brought in the finest specialists, took her to the most revered clinics, researched experimental drugs and procedures until one day she was just too tired to keep trying.

Not long after that, she slipped away.

Everyone attempted to console me but a loss like that is

too acute. There is nothing to be said or done to minimize the suffering.

After years of putting it out of my mind, the memories returned making sleep impossible and even unwanted. I was afraid of the dreams I might have.

Falling asleep after reading two books and the birds were beginning to chirp in the trees outside my bedroom window, when I awoke, my father and Lockie were gone.

I felt I failed again. Unable to offer my mother any comfort, that morning I had been unable to lie to Lockie as he left for the city. "All will be well," Julian of Norwich had said. In what well-ordered universe had she lived? All was rarely well.

Jules greeted me with sweet melon balls sprinkled with fresh chopped mint, and a soft-boiled egg.

I had no appetite.

"Worrying won't help," she said sitting across from me at the kitchen table.

"How did he look?"

"Fine. 'He was born with a gift of laughter and a sense that the world was mad.' How else could he be amused by Greer?"

"I wish she was . . ."

Jules spread some butter on a piece of raisin walnut bread she had made; excellent, but definitely improved by a good schmear of butter.

"What?"

"Nicer to him," I finished.

"You don't want her to be nice in her special way."

"Of course not, but must she scream at everyone? She's not a toddler."

"Greer doesn't know about his accident and I suspect she wouldn't care. Why should she remember that other people have problems when her own seem so urgent?"

"She's so spoiled."

"Yes."

"Why aren't you like that?"

"Talia!"

"You have a rich and powerful father. You grew up in Hollywood."

"Not Hollywood proper but yes, I know what you mean. I was always a shy, gangly girl."

"You outgrew that phase."

"See how there's hope for everyone? My father is like yours, very busy and important. People come to him for advice; they admire him."

"Is he admirable?"

"Yes, he is and so is your father." Jules stood and patted me on the shoulder.

"Don't say it'll be all right."

"I don't think you understand what that phrase means. It's not that everything will turn out as you wish, but that if you live with grace and dignity, you will be able to handle anything that comes your way. You've already demonstrated you can."

"And Greer can handle nothing."

"That's true."

Finishing what I could of the food in front of me, I went down to the barn. There was plenty to do and much to get done while Lockie was away for a few hours.

Greer was nowhere to be found, and there was no way I was getting up on her new horses, so I lunged Spare and Tracy lunged Counterpoint. By mid-morning, the stalls had been mucked and the horses had been brought in from the pastures. Right on time, 11 a.m., the morning's work was over.

I expected to hear from Lockie any moment telling me he was on the way home.

By noon, Jules and I had lunch of a delicious mozzarella and fresh tomato salad with grilled chicken breasts in the shade of the oak trees near the terrace. There was no peace and quiet as the lawn was being mowed. I still hadn't heard from Lockie.

"Do you want to go shopping with me?" Jules asked.

"No, thank you."

She reached for her cotton market bag from France that hung by the door. It was never enough to hold all she bought but Jules brought it out of habit. "Things always take longer with a doctor's visit than you imagine."

"Right. You go. I'll catch up on my reading."

"If you're not riding, you're reading."

"I promised myself I would read everything on the list for English lit for the fall semester. That way if I was busy, I wouldn't get behind."

"I'm sure Greer is doing the same thing. Not. How does some peach ice cream sound for dessert?"

"That would be fantastic."

"I'll go to the farm market and pick up some peaches and fresh corn and see what else they have."

Jules left and I remained on the terrace reading an old mystery. I was nearly finished with it when my cell phone rang.

I clicked it on. "Hello?"

"Hi. It's Lockie."

"I know that. I recognize your voice." By now, I would recognize his voice in a crowd of a thousand people. "Are you on the way home?"

There was a pause. "No. They want to keep me overnight and do some more tests."

"I can be there in two hours."

I immediately began planning the trip. We still had a car in the garage; I could take that to the city instead of my truck. Finding a garage that would accept a truck would be nearly impossible.

"Why would you do that?"

"You were alone last time. This time should be different."

"I'm fine."

"Don't say that."

"Tali, it's okay."

"It can't be if they're doing more tests."

"They're being thorough. I'm a new patient. You have to stay there and run the barn for me."

"Everything has been done. Pavel can do the afternoon chores without me."

"I don't want the barn unsupervised. Please stay and take care of it."

"When are you coming home?"

"Sometime tomorrow. As soon as I find out, I'll call. Then you can go shopping or have your own pedicure."

I didn't say anything.

"I'm teasing you. Geez, Tali. You can't go for the pedicure anyway since Derry Friel is coming to ride Greer's horses tomorrow. I take it she's not around today."

"She went sailing with a friend on Long Island Sound."

"That's a nice life she has," Lockie replied.

"She has no idea."

"No. Are you okay?"

"I'm not that okay."

"What will make it better?"

"Call me tonight."

"Fine. Before I go to sleep, I'll call."

"Thank you."

"Thank you."

We hung up and I keyed in my father's cell phone number.

"Hi, Talia, is there something wrong?"

"Why would you ask that?"

"You never call me."

"Things change. I need you to do something."

"Can it wait until the end of the business day?"

"You have to start now, or someone does, then yes, it can be this evening if you're staying in the city."

"Yes, I'm staying here. Did Lockie come back from the doctor's visit yet?"

"No. They're keeping him overnight. What I want you to do is take one of those iPads you have at the office and strip it of all the business stuff. Then get your assistant to load it with a variety of books and magazines for him to read. They don't have things like that at hospital. Make sure there's a copy of the Bible on it."

"Did he ask for this?"

"No. Does it sound like him that he would?"

"No. He's a true stoic."

"After you do all that, stop at a bakery or somewhere and get him a treat. Chocolate chip cookies, brownies, cupcakes. Something soft. Then go to the hospital and sit with him for an hour so he won't be alone."

"Maybe he doesn't want any company."

"So what?"

My father paused. "Wait. This is sounding familiar to me. This is what your mother would have done."

"Yes."

"All right. I'll take care of it."

I clicked off the phone, shut off my tablet and went back to the barn to start on the afternoon chores.

* * *

Around ten, Lockie called. My father had arrived with some small pastries and an iPad full of books in every genre. They talked about guy things until he left a few minutes ago when visiting hours were over. Lockie grilled me about what had gone on at the barn in his absence and it seemed as though I made everything happen as he wished. After thanking me, he said he'd see me the next day.

I still didn't feel good about it.

— 12 —

I WAS IN THE BARN THE NEXT MORNING when Derry Friel drove up and got out of his truck.

"Hi. Is Lockie around?"

"No, he's in the city."

"Who's his second in command?"

"Me. Talia Margolin."

"Hi. Lockie said he has some horses that need riding."

He had an Irish accent.

"Yes, ami-owner jumpers."

Derry pulled his saddle out of the truck. "Where's the ami-owner?"

"I have no idea. Does that make a difference?"

"I usually like to talk to the owner and find out what they want for the horse."

"We want you to ride Counterpoint and Spare. When Lockie's here he'll be very specific. My sister is . . . busy so you probably should consider them your project."

"Your sister. Is this your barn?"

"My father's."

"That's fine with me. Do you want me to ride them this morning?"

"I sure do."

"Anything I should know about them?"

"Nothing you won't find out after five minutes of being on top of them."

When he smiled, he was cute as a button as my grandmother would say.

Greer was going to like him. A lot. I felt as though the task of keeping them apart had just fallen on me. We needed him to ride the horses.

* * *

Around mid-afternoon a town car drove down the driveway, stopped and Lockie got out.

I could tell something was wrong by the way he walked toward me.

"Hi. What did the doctor say?"

"That I've reached the end of my career."

"How is your health?"

"Good. But the rest, not so bright. There's not much they can do since I plowed into a hard surface. It could have been much, much worse. I knew that from last year. I could have died or been paralyzed or brain damaged. Maybe I was."

"Lockie, don't say that."

"They're going to see if there's a better set of meds for the headaches. The doctor doesn't want me to compete anymore."

"That's no big deal."

"That's my life. I'm a good rider."

"You're a wonderful rider but you're an even better trainer. So what if you can't show?"

"I'm not sure you understand." Lockie paused for a long moment. "I'd like to be alone for a while. Is that okay?"

"I'm sorry, I didn't say it well."

"Our lives and possible futures are so different. You don't ever have to do anything and this is the only thing I can do or ever wanted to do and now I can't."

He turned and walked to the barn.

I stayed on the terrace and read without comprehending the words.

I knew he didn't mean it as an insult but what kind of person did it make me that an entire lifetime stretched ahead of me in which absolutely nothing was required? Simply because my father had money?

My mother certainly didn't think that was an excuse to be a slacker. There was much to be done in the world; people and animals needed to be helped. I had been blessed and never had the sense that gave me a pass to behave as irresponsibly and callously as Greer.

My father had been born into a very fortunate family and he never felt entitled to do nothing. He worked hard not only with his businesses but various charities.

I hoped that was just Lockie's disappointment being expressed and not what he believed was the truth about me.

About an hour later, I saw him lead Wing from the barn, get on the mounting block, settle into the saddle and ride down the into one of the pastures.

I didn't know what to say to him.

My mother would have known. She would have said it didn't matter as long as he was still alive.

He was fortunate to have dodged that bullet. My mother hadn't been so fortunate. I understood loss, too, intimately.

Jules came out with some cookies and iced tea. "Did Lockie come home?"

"He came back and it's not good."

Jules paused in mid-chew.

"No, he's fine but if I read between the lines, they don't want him to take chances of an accident like that ever happening again."

"That makes sense."

"He feels as though he has no future. Competing defined him in some way that I don't get and he knows that and I think I hurt his feelings."

"Lockie's one of the nicest people I've ever met and I've

met a lot of people. If he was upset after hearing the news, give him some time to process it. He'll be back to his normal self soon."

"He's right though, isn't he? Doesn't it change his life if he can't show?"

"Your life changed. My life has changed a couple times. Big changes. Unwanted changes. That's life. You can ignore it and pretend it's not happening as Greer tries so hard to do. She's miserable. She refuses to accept reality. Lockie will come to accept his reality."

"Which is what?"

"Was showing a part of what he was hired to do?"

"I don't know. Maybe."

"I don't see why this is a deal-breaker. Didn't Derry come here today and ride Greer's horses? Do you find people to ride horses at shows, too? Not everyone rides the horse they own. Not everyone shows the dogs they own. They hire someone to trot around Westminster Kennel Club with their dog. Go hire someone to show the horses you train."

"I suppose."

"Or you do it," Jules said.

I shook my head. "I don't plan on ever showing again. Now that my father has given up the idea that he could see Greer with the blue and me coming in second place, as usual, in the Maclay, why bother?"

Jules finished her cookie. "What do you think Lockie would like for dinner?"

"I have no idea."

It felt like a crack in the earth the size of the Ausable Chasm had just opened between us.

"Isn't that him riding in now? Why don't you go ask him and get back to me?"

"Oh. No. I don't think that's a good idea."

"Sure it is. Go ask."

I didn't move.

"I won't start dinner until I find out."

"You'd blackmail me? You'd hold my dinner hostage?"

"Of course I would."

I pushed back from the table and stood. "You must have learned how to be a tough negotiator from your father."

"I sure did."

There was no choice but to give up because at some point before midnight, I wanted to eat dinner. It seemed as though the walk to the barn was a mile long and I found him toweling Wing off after their ride.

"Jules sent me down to ask you what you want for dinner but that's just an excuse to force us to speak to each other."

"I like it here," Lockie said. "The reality is that my utility to your father has diminished dramatically."

"Did he say something?"

"No." Lockie didn't look at me, he just kept working on Wingspread.

"Then what makes you say that?"

"I was hired to get Greer to the finals. That's not happening. I was supposed to train horses. What's training without showing? You don't want to show. I can't show. Greer is undependable. What's my job? What's my value to this operation?"

"You still can train. Did they say you can't ride?"

"No, I can work on the flat but even that was a concession I had to pry out of them."

"So your head isn't going to explode. You can still stand or sit in the middle of the arena and tell me what to do. You can still run the barn, you can still train horses, and you're upset because you can't race across country full tilt and see if you can have another accident where you try to jam your spine into your brain stem a second time?"

— 13 —

LOCKIE STOOD UP AND LOOKED AT ME with an intensity I hadn't see in him before. "You have so fully comprehended the situation, Talia, I couldn't have said it better if I tried." He was angry.

I didn't blame him for that. Loss makes you temporarily insane.

"My mother is dead. I would give anything I have or will ever have if she was with me today under any circumstances. What you lost has already been replaced with many blessings. What do you want for dinner?"

Lockie thought for a long moment. "Beef."

"You want a steak?"

"Yes. And potatoes."

"Okay. But take a shower before you come up to the house, you're a mess."

He studied me. "What are you going to wear? Are you going out tonight?"

"That's not a bad idea. I'd like to go out tonight."

"Have a good time."

"Aren't you coming with me?"

"And be a third wheel?"

"Like a tricycle? What else has three wheels? Geez," I turned and walked out of the wash stall.

"Not a tricycle, Tali," he called after me.

"What then?" I paused and turned back around.

"The Messerschmidt cars have three wheels."

"That would still technically be a tricycle."

"A third leg then," Lockie replied.

"Like a stool?"

"If it has three legs."

"It wouldn't have two, that would make it a ladder."

"A ladder?" He looked at me as if I my brain had been fried in the summer heat. "What if it had four legs? Some stools have four."

"Four? Are we going on a double date?"

"This is a date?"

"I thought you wanted to be alone with me off the property. What the hell was that all about? We fly to Pennsylvania and we weren't alone anyway. I can't figure you out."

"Me? I said I wanted to be alone with you."

"So be alone with me tonight. What's so complicated about that?"

"Something obviously. What do you do in this town to go on a date?"

"The movies. Can you do that?"

"No. The lights and sound are too much. Besides, I don't want to be with you with clutter."

I wasn't following him at all. What did clutter mean? "Fine. Then we'll go to the state park and walk along the river and get bitten by mosquitoes. How does that sound?"

"Why don't we go get some ice cream?"

"Jules made you fresh peach ice cream."

"Why don't we just have ice cream here and walk to our own stream?" Lockie asked.

"You're impossible."

"I am very possible."

Lockie was back and I was so glad to see him, I nearly grabbed him the way I would have done with Butch.

* * *

I stopped halfway to the house and called my father.

"Are you coming home tonight?"

"No, I wasn't."

"I would like you to."

"Why?"

"I would like you to speak with Lockie."

"Wasn't that the reason telephones were invented so you didn't have to travel seventy-five miles to communicate?"

I said nothing.

"Your mother would have done it in person?"

"Yes."

"We're coming into an extremely busy season for me."

"This is important."

"I understand that and one day soon I'm going to explain why your mother knew how important our work was. Do you have any idea what I'm referring to?"

"Politics?"

"In general."

"Yeah, I'm not very interested in that."

"Your mother was. That's how we met. We were of one-mind on the subject."

"I find that hard to believe."

"Believe it. See you for dinner."

I couldn't see how it was possible for my mother to agree with my father on anything but the truth was I didn't know him very well.

After I was born, they didn't live together. I saw him infrequently and thought he was too busy for us. He had another family, I knew, and there was the very messy divorce. Even so, he was a good provider, and we had all we needed. As a child, I attended a private school and never met Greer who went to live with her mother for a while in England, which resulted in more legal actions.

Being young, and sheltered well, I didn't know many of the details. I suspect my mother and father continued to meet during the day while I was in school. The organization she worked for had something to do with him, tangentially. She told me she was in the information business. I was eight. I didn't ask.

Then once she became ill, I didn't ask.

After she died, I didn't want to know. And I had never asked because it was all over. For my mother, her job was done. Someone else must have stepped in. In some way, we are all very replaceable even when irreplaceable to a few people.

I went into the house and Jules looked up from the bread she was making.

"My father will be here for dinner."

"That's a surprise. Did you speak with Lockie?"

"Yes. He'd like a steak."

"Fine, we'll have filet mignon with brandy and mushroom cream sauce."

"He would like potatoes, too."

"I have new potatoes from the farm market. So everything is sorted out between you?" Jules glanced up from the dough she was kneading.

"It was more like arguing for a while. Then it was like . . ."

"What?"

"More arguing."

"What were you arguing about?"

"Where to go on a date," I said as I started to leave the room.

"Hang on. You can't say something like that and not finish."

"There isn't that much to say. We're not going out."

"Why not?"

"Because you're making ice cream and we have a stream."

"I don't understand."

"Me neither."

"He wanted to go out with you?"

"Why is that so shocking?"

"It's not shocking but you are the boss's daughter."

"I forgot about that." I started out of the room again. "And I forgot to tell him about Josh."

Jules stopped in mid-knead. "Talia."

"I know."

Going to my bedroom, I turned on the newest album by Michal Towber and lay down on my bed.

I had been seeing Josh for the last two years, if seeing was the correct word used for going out together given our circumstances. When I was new to The Briar School, Josh was one of the first in my class to welcome me. He was positioned somewhere in the middle between me, as stranger, and the rest of the students who were more like Greer.

Rogers was also somewhere in the middle, not sleek but

round, and unsure of what to do or say; never coordinated unless she was on a horse. A better rider than she thought, lack of confidence held Rogers back and her horse multiplied the problem.

Lockie would be a more effective teacher for her than Robert Easton, who had no patience and a very loud voice. I rode with him for half a lesson two years ago and walked out. He picked on Rogers, nearly mocking her at times, and she didn't have the wherewithal to tell him off and find another coach. Her parents pressured her to stay with him because Robert produced winners and up here in Litchfield County, everyone wanted to be a winner.

Except me.

* * *

My phone rang. I thought about letting it go to voicemail then looked at it and clicked on. "Hi."

"Hi. I just got a call from Marilyn and the skyscraper is leaving first thing tomorrow morning."

"That's good."

I had been looking forward to the grey horse's arrival. He seemed companionable and I missed the time spent going off into the woods with Butch to get away from everything. Maybe I would find that again with this horse.

I rode for pleasure. Greer rode for accolades. If she wasn't being praised, riding was a waste of effort.

There was a social aspect to showing that Greer enjoyed.

Most of her friends attended the same shows, had motor homes with well-stocked refrigerators they brought to the competitions and it was all very tail-gate partyish. They rode in the class, then put their horses in the vans and spent the rest of the time gossiping.

I wasn't a part of that social set, obviously. Greer's friends were not my friends. I didn't feel left out and was glad they didn't want anything to do with me.

"I asked her to send up that mare, too. Is that okay?"

"Lockie, it's your barn to run as you see fit. These are your decisions."

"I think she can be worked on for couple months and could be sold in October. That will give the buyer all winter to get used to her. I don't know what kind of plans you'd have for her."

"Stop it!"

"There are things that should be said."

"I don't know why," I replied.

"I had envisioned building an outside course this fall."

"So?"

"There's no one to train over it."

"You're still impossible."

"I'm possible."

"You have too high an opinion of yourself in that case."

"Tali."

"What?"

"I think I should talk to your father and offer to leave."

I felt like tossing the phone across the room. "Hey, this is working out perfectly because he's on his way up to the city to talk to you."

"What does he want to say?"

"I have no idea. It's between the two of you."

"Do you really not know?" Lockie was too clever not to have suspicions.

"What difference does it make? You made your decision. You want to leave."

"I don't want to leave but it's not fair to the farm to stay when I can't do everything I was hired to do."

"I have to take a shower before dinner but I just want to ask one question."

"That sounds like a setup."

"Did you take job figuring you could ignore your headaches and the photosensitivity and go back to riding pretending everything was fine?"

He didn't answer for a moment.

"Yes or no. No's as good an answer as yes."

"Yes. Carefully."

"That was so unfair."

"That's why I think I should leave."

"Unfair to yourself. Go take a shower. It's almost time for dinner."

"Talia?"

"Bye." I hung up.

How badly did he need this job to risk his health, future and life?

I pulled off my jeans and went into my bathroom.

He said he would be paying off the hospital bill for years. He sold his horse. He had little more than his tack when he arrived here.

Had he tried to get other jobs down south and been rejected because everyone there knew about the accident?

Lockie had assessed the situation accurately. A top stable would expect him to show. He was a combined training rider. Even if he had become a strictly equitation teacher, he would be expected to show hunters for the publicity value.

Lockie was somewhat famous. Not to the world at large but in the equestrian world, he was. He had enormous talent; at fifteen, Lockie had competed against adults in the open jumper division and beaten them. Even if he was based in California, he came East for the big shows. He had been on the Winter Circuit in Florida.

Everyone wanted him to ride their horses. It was termed catch riding. He'd be at a show and an owner or trainer would want someone super talented to ride their horse in a class.

It took an unusual rider to get on a horse, warm it up and take it into the ring with an expectation of winning. Lockie was that good. As a junior.

Everyone in the horse show community was talking

about him. It wasn't possible to read *The Chronicle of the Horse* without seeing his picture every few weeks.

Then after he went to the Ruhlmann's and concentrated on combined training, Lockie was less interesting to that hunter/jumper crowd. I stopped hearing about him. If I had thought about it, the assumption would have been that he went to Europe where stadium jumping was a major sport. In America, no one outside the horse world knew what it was.

Turning on the water, I stepped under the spray.

I understood why Lockie thought his life as he knew it was over. It was. No Olympics. No international competitions.

But that was hardly signified the end of his life and accommodations could be made. It was just a change in plans. An alternate future.

All I could do was hope my father would say the right things. I still didn't trust him and knew how easily my father could disappoint me.

After toweling off, I changed three times before hitting on the right combination. Not into clothes the way Greer was, I relied almost completely on Jules to go shopping with me, and pick out appropriate outfits. She had wonderful sense of style but how could she not given where she had grown up.

Hurrying downstairs because as I predicted, quite correctly, that I would be late.

We were eating on the terrace, something that was more Jules' choice than mine, since dining al fresco in the evening was normal in her family but we had bugs in Connecticut and I hated slapping at mosquitoes instead of eating.

"Hi, sorry," I said, sitting down quickly.

"Now we can have dinner?" My father started on his salad.

"I don't want to spoil the meal," Lockie began.

"Then don't," I replied.

My father let his fork drop onto the plate. "Let's get to it then we can eat."

"I'm offering to quit. I understand I have a contract and if you wanted to get rid of me, one of your lawyers could do it in five minutes but you shouldn't be forced into that position."

My father looked at me then to Lockie. "Why would you quit?"

"His doctor wasn't . . ." I started.

"I can do this without help."

"He didn't vet out sound," I finished.

— 14 —

"THANK YOU VERY MUCH, Tali, I was doing it my way."

"You were taking too long."

"Learn some patience. Tempo. Pace. Think around the corner."

Jules tapped her water glass with her fork to get our attention. "Not at the dinner table."

Lockie gave me a look that was easy to translate. Back off. "I was hired to fulfill certain job specs and I can't, so you should be free to be able to find someone who can."

"This is amazing," my father said and looked at each of us. "This is why you had me come up from the city?"

"Yes."

"Tali," Lockie said. "Stop running my life."

"Stop ruining your life and I will."

"Time out. Can I get a word in edgewise?"

I turned to my father. "Of course."

"Lockie, I spoke to your doctor yesterday and today. I'm fully aware of your condition. You have a contract, you're staying. Now can we eat in peace?"

"It's all good to me," I said and picked up my fork.

"And," my father continued, "the doctor said there are some experimental photochromic contact lenses being made in Singapore. They should help with the light sensitivity problem. So now your biggest problem is dealing with Talia. Let me give you a hint, she's just like her mother and I didn't have a prayer with Sarah."

"Thank you, sir, all advice is gratefully accepted." He turned to me. "Don't kick me under the table."

* * *

Dessert was freshly churned peach ice cream scooped into homemade Italian style waffle cones. Lockie and I took them from Jules then headed through the pastures to the stream where we sat on an outcropping of rocks left over from the Ice Age and couldn't lick fast enough to prevent being dripped on.

"That friend of yours," Lockie began.

There was a long pause.

"Rogers," I supplied.

"Yes, Rogers. Would you please call and invite her to a lesson at her earliest possible convenience?"

"Sure. Should she bring her horse?"

"No, let's have her ride the German mare."

"Okay."

"You sound unsure."

"Rogers doesn't have a great deal of confidence."

"Can she ride?"

"She's been riding her whole life."

"She'll be fine."

I finished my ice cream then went to the stream to wash my hands in the water. "There's something I've been meaning to tell you."

"Avoiding telling me, it sounds like."

"We've all been invited to an anniversary party this weekend. It's a big celebration every year; they hold nothing back. There's at least one band, professional fireworks, photographers, videographers, journalists to write it all up so the common folk can feel left out."

Lockie said nothing.

"Tents, dance floor, catered food. You won't find hot dogs there."

"That's a relief."

"I go with someone from school, the son of the anniversary couple. I always . . ."

"Have a good time." Lockie stood and began walking back to the barn.

"You're supposed to go."

"Fireworks give me a headache. Light and noise. It's too much."

We walked back in silence. At the barn, Lockie said a quick goodnight and left me standing there.

I don't know what I expected but not this reaction.

After reading late into the night, when I turned out my light, his was already out.

* * *

At just after 2 p.m. the next day, the horses arrived from Pennsylvania. Freudigen Geist walked me into the barn not noticing I was on the other end of the lead rope and he was even larger than I remembered him.

For a moment, it occurred to me that I may have made a mistake. Was I going to be over-mounted on him? I remembered Lockie standing there in the Theissens' indoor saying "this is a really big horse, Talia." Was the translation "this is too much horse for you" and I didn't get it?

I had liked the grey gelding then. He was comfortable and Lockie had been right that there was a sense of security but now I wondered if I was going to be dragged everywhere. If he started to misbehave, would I be strong enough to control him?

Butch never tested me and we were so compatible. This horse looked over the top of my head and didn't see me below him. If I didn't make sure he knew I was stronger willed than he was, there would be no end to the problems. Horses might not have a genius IQ but they were plenty clever when the need arose.

Fortunately, Greer had left the house late that morning to join friends for a pool party so there was no commentary from her to deal with. She had worked with Lockie on Counterpoint in the morning over fences that were too big for me to contemplate. Then they spent time on Spare and I was impressed since I was unable to remember her ever working that hard. If Lockie had arrived in February, maybe she would have made it to the National Horse Show.

That her equitation career was finished didn't seem to bother Greer one whit. She had always derived more of a charge from going at top speed, hence the Porsche and the collection of warnings from the local cops. Lockie had figured her out when everyone else had been unable to do so.

By the end of the day, I couldn't stand it any longer and cornered him in the tack room.

"Are you going to talk to me ever again?"

"Of course. I didn't realize I wasn't talking to you."

"I'm going out for dinner," I started.

"Have a good time."

"Stop it! I'm going out with Rogers to give her the courage to tell her parents she wants to ride with you."

"That's fine. Thanks. Why don't you get up on the mare tomorrow and see how she is. Have Tracy help you if you need it."

"Where are you going to be?"

"I got a call from the doctor and the contact lenses were overnighted from Singapore so that's what I'm doing. Then I'm going to stop and visit some people in Bedford. They invited me to dinner and since I haven't seen them in a long time, at least a year, it sounded like a good idea. It's okay if I keep the car and driver that long?"

Lockie had problems driving at night with the oncoming headlights.

"No, that's not a problem."

My mother was always so patient with me, and my father insisted I was so much like her but right then I didn't feel like her, I felt like my father, who usually had a pretty short fuse.

"Thank you. Then I'll see you Saturday. Although probably not, on second thought."

"What are you talking about?"

"Your big shindig."

"Yeah. Exactly. Going to the ol' shindig. Well, you have fun in Bedford."

"I will."

Nearly hissing at him, I walked back to the house, went into the kitchen and stuck my head under the sink faucet, letting the cold water pour over me.

"What happened to you?" Jules asked.

"I'm not eating with him tonight. Thankfully."

"I'll eat with him; I think he's adorable."
I practically hissed at her, too.

— 15 —

IT WASN'T HARD TO CONVINCE Rogers giving up on Robert was a net gain and we concocted a reason why it would be so much more convenient to ride with Lockie. She promised she would tell them the next morning or afternoon, whenever they ambled across her path.

The following day, Lockie was already gone when I reached the barn, but there had been no a big rush to get there. I rode the mare and thought she would be a wonderful horse for Rogers. Comfortable and gentle, she was well-trained, bomb-proof and Rogers would learn an enormous amount by riding her. I always thought it was a mistake for her to own a Thoroughbred. Her gelding tended to be so scatty and unpredictable, Rogers never knew what to expect. This made it impossible for her to relax which made the horse even more nervous. It was a never-ending supply of fail.

Butch and I went on a trail ride for an hour doing nothing more than walk. Going back to the house, Jules and I went shopping for the party.

While Newbury was a small town, there were a few stores that catered to the weekend residents who expected the same quality of goods that they could find in the city. The quality might have been the same but the selection was much smaller.

"I wonder," I started as we walked down the sidewalk.

"Then call him," Jules said over me.

"How do you know what I'm talking about?"

She opened the door to a boutique and we went inside. "You're right I don't. I assumed you were wondering how Lockie was doing being fitted for his fancy contact lenses."

"I was wondering if Josh had come home yet."

"Liar." Jules laughed as she headed deep into the shop where the fancier dresses were kept.

"Josh has been a good friend to me."

"Yeah?" Jules began going through a rack and held a dress out to me. "This is really cute."

"So what?"

"Try it on."

"Why can't I wear what I wore last year? Why can't I wear something of yours?"

"Okay." She pushed her bags into my arms. "I'm trying it on."

I followed her to the back where there was a former closet transformed into a dressing room. Jules banged around in there for a moment then the door opened and she was half-dressed.

"Are they kidding me? It's not big enough for a Barbie doll to get dressed in there. Act as a screen and we'll pretend no one can see me."

I moved in front of Jules to prevent anyone walking on the street who happened to look in the window at that moment from finding it possible to see her in the back of the shop.

"You're so much better as a sister than Greer," I commented over my shoulder.

"That I believe."

"Don't leave."

"I'm not going anywhere. Actually, I am, but you should come with me. I'm going to LA in the fall for a week to see my parents."

"I go to school, remember?"

"If that's the reason, stay home."

"Yeah, I'll go with you."

I turned, zipped her up and she studied herself in the mirror. "You'll look terrific in this."

So I bought it.

* * *

Josh called that night as I was about to go to sleep. He had just arrived home for the party and had much to tell me about touring with the road company. He was talking so fast, I couldn't follow what he was saying and simply looked out the window.

The light wasn't on in Lockie's apartment. He hadn't returned yet.

* * *

I took the day off and didn't go to the barn; Greer did it often enough, why was I expected to be there every moment of my life?

Unfortunately, being at the barn was my life and I didn't have a blooming thing to do otherwise.

Rogers called and said she told her parents she was leaving Robert and going to ride with Lockie. They said "Fine, dear," and headed out for lunch at the country club. I told her that was terrific and we talked for a half hour about nothing then we both had to start getting ready.

Jules French braided my hair because if it was good enough for a horse, it was good enough for me. Then I pulled the dress over my head, it was cute—pinks and purples in layers. Jules loaned me some purple heels she had and I wanted my jeans and paddock boots back so decided to wear trainers until arriving at the party.

Jules dressed in a stylish pale green cocktail dress and did nothing with her hair but let it cascade over her shoulders. She was beautiful whether she was in a $2000 dress or splashed with spaghetti sauce.

My father called early in the day and said he had to fly out to Wisconsin on important business so Jules and I were on our own. We drove to the Standish estate in my truck. Normally I would have checked on the horses, but was sure Lockie had all of it well in hand.

"Will you do me a favor?" Jules said as we drove into the field serving as a parking lot for all the Standish guests.

"Sure."

"Solve this disagreement with Lockie by Monday."

"Why does it fall on me?" I asked getting out of the truck.

"Because it's about you, isn't it?"

"Yes."

"Unless you don't want it solved. You only have a couple more weeks of summer and then you'll be seeing Josh every day. You'll fall back into the old routine. I'm sure it's comfortable."

I tried to figure out whether she thought it was good to be comfortable with Josh or not as we proceeded to the largest tent where the band was playing.

Soon we had drinks and found a place to sit. A few minutes later, a friend of Jules' arrived and after making sure I'd be fine, she left to mingle.

Leaving sounded very appealing as I was not party-minded right then, but Josh expected me to be there and I would do things for him I wouldn't do for others. Finally, he tapped me on the shoulder and kissed my cheek.

"Hi! I'm glad you made it."

"How could I miss this party?" I replied glancing around at all the society types drifting like swans through the crowd.

"It is pretty grim, isn't it?"

I nodded.

Every year was the same. Over the top food, drink, decorations and guests. Then his parents toasted each other in the completely hearty though insincere fashion expected for the occasion. I didn't know if they loved each other or not, but they were a prominent local couple so there was always something for them to do together and there was no sense in getting a divorce if they didn't.

"The fireworks are never less than excellent," I admitted. "Tell me about the tour. It must have been fun traveling from town to town, like being with the circus."

Josh pushed back the lock of hair that usually fell into his face. It was winningly boyish but he didn't want to be considered a kid anymore, he wanted to be adult. The suggestion to use mousse to hold his hair in place if it bothered him so much must have bothered him more because he refused. I thought someone accustomed to wearing makeup on stage wouldn't have a emotional breakdown over a little glop on his hair but no.

"Everyone should go on a road tour once," he said. "Even if it's only to experience every Shanty Shack Motel in the country."

"Does that mean you don't want to do it again?"

"I liked the acting but not the traveling," Josh confessed and for the next hour, he regaled me with stories of being on the road and on the stage.

With quite a talent for entertaining, maybe he should work at it with more concentration than he had during freshman through junior years in high school. I doubted that his parents would be happy with that choice of careers. They wanted him to go into investment banking since it ran in the family like his floppy hair. His older brother was already majoring in finance at Carnegie Mellon.

I felt a hand on my shoulder and looked up to see who it was.

— 16 —

"EVERYONE SAYS THIS ISN'T A PARTY TO BE MISSED."

"Who said?"

"Greer."

He held out his hand to Josh. "Lockie Malone."

"Josh Standish." Josh looked questioningly at me.

"Lockie is our new trainer," I explained.

"How much longer are you going to keep doing that horse showing thing? I thought you hated it."

Lockie pulled up a chair close to mine then sat. "Something else you didn't tell me?"

"Didn't Greer tell you?" I was ready to go home and dinner hadn't been served yet.

"She didn't have to. I figured it out for myself."

We sat there in uncomfortable silence for a few minutes."

Lockie leaned back in his chair. "So you're his beard and he's what? The reason why you can't have a relationship with a guy?"

"Josh is my friend," I replied in annoyance.

"I'm not ready to make an announcement from the rooftops," Josh said quite calmly considering the stark truth of it.

"When I came to the school, I was an outsider and both Rogers and Josh welcomed me. I didn't have any other friends. I still don't."

"Thank you for taking care of her," Lockie said to Josh, took my hand, stood and pulled me to my feet.

"I'll talk to you later," I told Josh.

"Don't worry about it; I'm glad you found someone. I was going to tell you tonight that so did I." Josh gave me his half smile and shrug.

I was pulled out a side exit to the lawn. "Lockie, what's this about?"

"Now we're far enough away from the band and you can dance with me."

"This is about dancing?"

"Dancing is an excuse to press one body up against another." He took me in his arms and we began moving to the music.

It was more than I could have imagined it to be.

Through the fine fabric of the dress, I could feel the heat of his body against mine. His thighs against mine, his chest against my chest, his arm wrapped across my back holding me so close there was not an ion of airspace between us.

"I don't understand. What do you want?"

"If I really have a say in the matter, I want you to treat me the way you treat Butch."

I laughed. "You want me to take the trimmers to your ears?"

"If my ears need it, yes."

"I'm not cleaning your sheath, that's something you should do for yourself."

Lockie pulled me still closer. "Maybe I can talk you into it," he whispered into my ear."

"No."

"I'm very persuasive." He paused. "I already got you switched from equitation to dressage."

"Not that much of a triumph. I usually use the hose and cold water. Does that sound appealing?"

"I don't believe you."

"Why not?"

"For Butch? You'd be sticking your elbow in the water to make sure it was just the right temperature."

"You're not Butch."

"You could pretend until it comes naturally to you. This is the first time I'm saying that to you but it won't be the last."

"I don't pretend."

"You pretended with Josh."

"If someone makes an assumption, what does that have to do with me?"

"Tali. You did everything but with him. Be honest."

"I owed him."

"You don't owe me anything." He sighed into my ear. "You will."

"You owe me."

"All right. I owe. That's my life. Can we go home now? It's loud and the lights are starting to come on."

I pulled back. "What about the contact lenses? Aren't you wearing them?

"There's a schedule so my eyes can adapt to them."

"Okay, we'll go. I have to tell Jules. No, I'll call her. How did you get here?"

"I got a ride with Greer. She drives very fast. She can drive with one hand, too." He pulled me back to him. "She put her right hand on my leg and was heading north."

"What did you do?"

"Are you kidding? I said 'Come to me, baby!'"

"Last time a guy tried that with me I said 'Move your hand or you're going to need a tourniquet for what's left.'"

"I guess you didn't want the attention." He let me go.

"Good guess."

From the wrong guy, it's always unwanted attention. From the right guy, it's a request.

We began walking toward the parking lot.

"Lockie!" A tall blond appeared out of nowhere, practically launched herself at him and kissed him full on the lips. "Why haven't you called me?"

She was more than moderately pretty, thin, tanned and obviously a rider. Her very fine hair gathered on top of her head looked like the spiky petals of a flower. It was a smart choice and a solution she must have worked out a while ago for these occasions. There wasn't much else she could do.

I looked at him.

He looked back at me and shook his head slightly.

I held out my hand to her. "I'm Talia Margolin from Bittersweet Farm."

"I'm Alise Farrow. I'm the new trainer at Dinglebrook Farm."

"Over in Middlebury."

"Yes. It's a wonderful facility with a huge indoor, a cross country course and an arena with stadium jumps. We have everything you could hope for including some very talented horses."

Dinglebrook was a top tier commercial barn. Our farm was private, for our use. We never needed to reproduce the Kentucky Horse Park in the backyard.

I looked back at Lockie and he shook his head again.

"I didn't know where you were," Lockie said.

"Now that you do, let's get together. We have some nice horses and a course through the woods and fields that's so much like Knoleton, you can hardly tell the difference. Do you still have your horse?"

"Yes. Wingspread's with me."

"What a great horse. But you haven't been doing much with him."

"The Ruhlmanns had him for a while because I was . . ."

"Busy," I said.

Lockie nodded.

"It was so nice to meet you, Alise, and we'll give you a call as soon as we have some free time and we'll come for a visit," I said.

Her smile faded then returned. "That would be fantastic! See you!" She leaned over and kissed him again then zipped away.

"I have no idea who that was," Lockie said as we continued to my truck.

"She knows you."

"What was her name?"

"Alise."

Lockie shook his head.

"There's some peach ice cream left over."

"Any cones? Those were good."

"Maybe. I better change."

"Don't."

"Why not? I don't want to drip on this dress."

"You look . . ." he paused. "Fetching."

I drove home, found the ice cream in the freezer and managed to get two good sizes portions out of what was left. We went onto the terrace and sat on the glider together eating ice cream and watching the lightning bugs in the field below us.

After an hour, he stood up. "See you tomorrow. I want you to ride the grey horse."

"You're not going to kiss me goodnight?"

"No."

"Any reason?"

"Besides that you're the boss's daughter?"

"Besides that."

"I'm playing hard to get."

"Okay." I could hear him almost laughing.

He began walking down the path then stopped. "Why do you stay up so late?"

"I'm afraid of the dreams I might have."

"Maybe that will change. Goodnight, Tali."

"Goodnight, Lockie."

— 17 —

I HAD A NEARLY IMPOSSIBLE time falling asleep. All I could think of was Greer putting her hand on his thigh. She probably used her finger to trace along his inside seam. It was what she always did. I knew this because Greer explained it to her friend, Sabine, one morning on the way to a horse show and I had been an unwilling captive in the car.

Greer must be looking for a new playmate.

Did it have to be Lockie?

* * *

"Leave him alone, Greer," I said to her the next morning as she filled her brushed stainless steel container with coffee.

"What are you talking about now?"

136

"Everything is going perfectly for you. You have a terrific trainer and two wonderful horses. If you want Lockie to coach you to the Winter Circuit, don't get him fired."

"No one's getting fired for a little pat and tickle."

"You won't stop at that," I replied.

"I do get carried away. I'm not a committed virgin like you are. I'm not . . . cold. Although I supposed that appeals to some men. I guess Josh likes the distance between you."

Jules wrapped two danish pastries in waxed paper and put them in the wicker basket used to transport food to Lockie.

I didn't like Greer before but now I was starting to loathe her.

"I take after my mother," Greer said. "And you take after yours."

I wanted to punch her.

"My mother can get any man she wants," Greer said screwing the lid onto her coffee container.

"She can get them but she can't keep them," I replied.

"You are a bitch of the first order," Greer said.

"You're a slut," I said in all honesty.

"That's enough," Jules said.

Greer glared at me. "I have a lesson this morning. Lockie will teach me about riding and then I'll teach him about . . ." she gave me a coquettish toss of her shoulders "riding."

I picked up an apple from the fruit bowl, threw it and hit her shoulder. If only it had been a little higher, maybe it would have broken her nose.

Greer smiled and left the house in her skin-tight low-rise breeches and her tan field boots.

"Don't let her get to you," Jules said.

"I don't know what to do."

"Tell me about it."

I put my hand on the basket. "There's nothing to tell, really. She's poison."

"She does have a way about her," Jules admitted.

"You must have met women like this in Hollywood."

"Oh yeah."

"What do you do?"

"This is not what you want to hear but you have to do nothing."

"Nothing?" I asked in disbelief.

"Be you. Do your thing. Be the daughter your mother would be proud of. That's what you can do."

"She doesn't know how badly she can hurt him."

Jules reached out and rubbed my arm. "Dolcezza. Have faith in him. Lockie's not your father."

I looked into her beautiful hazel eyes.

Jules nodded. "Trust me on this." She took my hand and squeezed it. "Really."

"I don't want to see him hurt."

"That's one of your most endearing qualities."

"I'd like to see her hurt, so don't be so endeared," I replied.

She leaned over and kissed my cheek. "It will be okay."

"Not okay in the it turns out how I want it to way but okay in the I come to accept more bad things happening way."

"I wouldn't put it like that."

"No, you wouldn't."

"Get down there and give him some breakfast. I made him a nice egg and ham sandwich."

"Thank you."

"Go. It's getting cold."

I walked down to the barn and since Greer had driven the thousand feet, she was already on Counterpoint, warming him up in the outdoor ring.

Watching as she cantered him easily around the track, I couldn't help but admire her skill. Her position was perfect, almost unnatural, it so conformed to the requirements. When she wanted something, Greer did apply herself to getting it and for the last three years, all she wanted was to win the Medal and the Maclay.

In a way, I felt sorry for her. I knew what it was like to be disappointed, although I very much doubted whether it bothered us for the same reasons or in the same manner.

"Hi, Tal," Lockie said coming up behind me. He was wearing his darkest sunglasses, not a good sign.

"Jules sent some food and tea."

He hesitated.

"You have to try to eat at regular intervals. I know you don't feel like it but you can't play around with your blood sugar. It will cause headaches."

"It's not good this morning."

"Did you take your meds?"

"Yes." He was about to take the basket from me then decided against it.

Greer pulled up in the middle of the ring. "I'm waiting."

"I had a fight with her so she's not in a good mood. I'm sorry."

"I'll work her hard for twenty minutes and by the end of the session, she'll have had enough of me."

He was so wrong about that.

"Go get the grey horse ready, okay?"

"Sure."

He slipped between the planks and entered the arena.

I went into the barn to visit with Butch and get ready for my own lesson.

We spent the entire twenty minutes at a sitting trot with Lockie trying to teach me how to use my back and seat. I had been riding for most of my life and none of this was ever been mentioned to me before.

Lockie seemed quieter than usual and even though we were in the indoor, he was still wearing his glasses. I wondered if I was disappointing him. Now with a well-trained horse, maybe I wasn't a very good rider and he wasn't free to say that.

"Walk. And hold him together. It's not a trail ride."

I pulled the gelding to a walk.

"That's good. Nice pace."

I turned into the center of the ring. "What's wrong?"

"I think it falls under the heading of my meds need to be adjusted."

"I'm sorry."

"It'll take a while to get it right. Would you use my dressage saddle tomorrow?"

I didn't reply.

"Tali, the close contact saddle is not helping you."

"It's one more thing to get used to," I replied.

"Name the other ones."

"Joy."

"You're calling him Joy?"

"I am because that's his name—Joyful Spirit. Freudigen Geist."

"You should call him The Chrysler Building. He's the same color."

"You really don't feel any better." I could see it in the way he stood, in the way he moved, as if everything hurt.

"No."

"Rogers is supposed to be here any minute, do you want me to try to call and cancel?"

"No, it hasn't been an hour yet." He pushed the sunglasses further up to the bridge of his nose.

"Is there anything that triggers the headaches or does it just happen?"

"Sometimes I think it's the weather but not always. Don't worry about it."

"You said you wanted me to treat you like Butch."

"What would you do for Butch?"

"Sit in the stall with him telling him how handsome he'd look with daisies braided through his mane."

Lockie smiled. "I'm sure that would make him feel much better."

"Why don't you go upstairs and lay down for a few minutes."

"Yeah, I think I will. And if Rogers arrives, get her up on the horse and lunge her for a couple minutes. I'll be down in about twenty minutes. Okay?"

"Sure."

"Lockie!" Greer rushed into the indoor arena through the main entrance.

"Yes, Greer?"

"I thought we were working on Spare this morning."

"That's tomorrow. The farrier is coming this morning because he has a loose shoe."

She approached him, walking her walk. Something made her think it was sexy and alluring. Maybe someone in a movie walked that way and got the guy in the end. Or maybe it was in a music video. If she had to advertise, why not just get a tee-shirt printed up with big letters detailing what she wanted.

"I could ride Sans."

To listen to her without the paying attention to the words, you'd think she was making an offer of something much different. She wouldn't attempt to run this routine on Lockie if it hadn't worked with other guys and produced the desired results.

"Why?" I asked quite sensibly.

"Because I want to be a better rider now that I have a better coach." Stepping so close to him, Greer was nearly on Lockie's feet.

"Thank you, that's a very nice compliment but I have a couple phone calls to make to try to sell your horse. You have the day off."

"You selling Sans?" Her tone changed instantly.

"Your father instructed me to do so."

"I need a backup!"

"Greer, you have Counterpoint and Spare's your backup. You don't need an equitation horse," I said.

She looked at me in disdain. "Is that your new horse?"

"Yes."

"He's built like a dump truck."

"He has perfect conformation for a Hanoverian," Lockie said stepping away from her and heading toward the side door.

"A Hanoverian dump truck," Greer retorted. Then she shook her head as if I was hopeless. "If that's what you want, go figure."

"This is what I want."

"Fine, you wouldn't catch me dead on that thing. What an embarrassment. I'm going to Sabine's if anyone wonders where I am," Greer said.

"They won't," I replied as she left.

I dismounted, untacked Joy and brought him into the wash stall for a quick rinse even though he was barely damp. Obviously, twenty minutes of work didn't make a big impression on him and I returned him to his stall. He would have a very nice life here with very little asked of him.

Out behind the barn I found some red clover the lawnmowers had missed, picked the blossoms and went upstairs to the apartment.

"Lockie." I tapped on the door.

"It's open."

— 18 —

HE WAS LYING ON THE SOFA.

That would be my next project, redecorating this apartment for him. It had been this way since I had come to live at the farm; the time was past due for fresh paint and decent furniture. He needed a sofa long enough so his legs didn't hang over the armrests.

"Is Rogers here?"

"Not yet." I sat on the coffee table next to him. "I couldn't find any daisies but I found some clover." I slid a stem by his ear.

"Am I handsome now?"

"Very."

"Because we can't let ourselves go even if we are retired."

Lockie's smile was so small it almost required a magnifying glass to see.

"You sneak! Are you listening to everything I say to Butch?"

"It's not as though you were whispering in his ear so only he could hear."

It wasn't the first time someone pointed out that I did carry on a running, one-sided conversation with the horses. "I don't want you to make fun of me."

"Tali, I wouldn't do that."

"You found it amusing."

"Yes," he admitted.

"So you were laughing at me."

"No, I am . . . charmed by your relationship with Butch. You know that. Don't misinterpret what I'm saying. I'm handsome now."

"Wow." I watched as his eyes closed. "Did the meds just kick in?"

"Yes."

I had seen that look before. My mother said it was like falling back into a cloud.

"They're strong, aren't they?"

He opened his eyes and made the effort to focus. "Very."

I removed the clover from his hair. "Come on, we'll go downstairs and you'll sit in the middle of the ring. If you need to have any jumps moved or rails changed, I'll do it."

"Thank you."

"Just this once because . . ."

"I already owe you," he finished.

"That's completely correct."

He stood up slowly.

This was just like my mother had been those last months. The medications were so strong to deal with the pain that she was always light-headed, dizzy and half-awake.

"I'll be okay in a few minutes. Once it all stabilizes. My glasses," he said and I grabbed them off the table.

"Why aren't you wearing the contacts?"

"Tali."

"You're getting used to them."

"Yes."

On the aisle, Tracy had the mare with her bridle on, waiting for Rogers to arrive with her own saddle and a moment later Rogers walked in. I saw her pause as she saw Lockie, then she walked forward almost reluctantly.

"Hi, Rogers," Lockie said. "It's good to see you again."

She blushed. "Hi."

I almost couldn't hear her and felt like giving her a swift kick to her butt.

"Let's get her tacked up," I said as Tracy appeared with a saddle pad and girth. A few minutes later, I had Rogers in the saddle and walking into the ring.

"Why are we indoors?" She said softly to me.

"Because getting too much sun makes you look old before your time."

"That's a good reason."

I was pleased the excuse had come to me so quickly.

"This is going to be an easy day, Rogers," Lockie told her as he walked in a small circle, following her on the track. "I want you to get used to the mare and let her get used to you. And, of course, get used to me," he said with a smile. He was feeling better.

The characteristic Lockie shared with my mother was their ability to put aside whatever they were going through and focus on someone else. I remembered telling my mother "Stop worrying about me." She'd ask about school, my trip to it and back, and whatever I had done afterwards. Curious, she wanted to know about everything whether it was my homework or the latest gossip. I couldn't remember ever hearing her complain or feel sorry for herself. Instead, she felt sorry for me, for what the illness had taken away from my childhood that should have been so carefree and without worry.

Maybe my life should have been different but that wasn't the life I was destined to have. Even my father couldn't change that. I tried to make everything as easy as possible for her. I hoped I succeeded once in a while.

That morning I thought she would recognize some of her qualities in Lockie.

"Pick up the pace a little, Rogers. Brisk trot."

The last time I saw Rogers ride, the horse had run off with her and scared the peanuts out of her M&M's. Her parents thought Sinjon was a wonderful horse since he looked like the old oil painting on the wall above the living room fireplace. She was afraid to tell them she was afraid to ride him.

I knew he cost a ton of money and had been bought at one of the top show stables on the East Coast. Robert probably made thousands under the table on the sale.

It was understandable that an instructor would get a finder's fee from the seller if the right buyer was brought into the mix. I understood that was how business worked. Everyone knew when Robert was involved, the price of the horse would be jacked up higher than normal.

He was greedy, arrogant and successful. People forgive many faults if they get what they want in the end. Robert was absolved of all his indiscretions; winning was that important. Winning was status and sometimes money; not prize money, but the sales price of a horse could get a boost with the right win.

Watching Rogers attempt to follow all of Lockie's instructions, I wondered if she was as unhappy showing as I was but, unlike me, was unwilling to say the words. That I didn't like showing was a secret to no one who knew me for more than a couple weeks.

After fifteen minutes on the flat, a good portion of it

working at a collected trot, Lockie had Rogers pop over a few fences. I knew that was a lot to ask but when she saw the fences were only about two feet high, it was less intimidating.

The mare would have jumped anything she was pointed at, I was certain of that, and Rogers made it around flawlessly. She was beaming when the lesson ended. Pulling the mare to a halt, Rogers patted her neck and looked to Lockie.

"When's the next lesson?"

"How about Friday?"

"How about Wednesday?"

"You should practice for a few days on your own horse and then come back," Lockie replied.

Rogers stopped smiling.

"What just happened?" Lockie asked immediately.

I stepped closer to him so Rogers couldn't hear. "She's terrified of her horse."

"I should have gone to college and become a psychiatrist," he said quietly. "My grades were good, but no, I had to go into equestrian sports."

"Wednesday's fine, Rogers," I told her.

"Tali," Lockie began.

"I have an idea," I said.

"Wednesday and Friday. Does that sound good, Rogers?" Lockie asked.

"Thank you!" She was beaming again as she rode the horse out of the indoor.

"Would you do me a favor?" I asked him.

"Since I owe you, as you've reminded me a number of times, I can't say no to anything, can I?"

"Good point. Would you go up to the house and have some iced tea on the terrace?"

"Why?"

"I haven't seen you drink anything in the last hour."

He was about to say something.

"You said you wanted me to treat you like Butch."

"I forgot that. I'll go up to the house. Are you sure you don't need a lead rope to get me there?"

"Haven't you ever seen me call Butch out of the field first thing in the morning? He follows me right into the barn without a lead rope. If he can find his stall, you can find the terrace."

"I'm smarter than he is."

"You'll have to prove it. As soon as Rogers leaves, I'll meet you up there for lunch."

I watched him walk away. If I was really treating him like Butch, I would have at least kissed him goodbye on the muzzle.

— 19 —

ROGERS WAS MORE EXCITED than a six year old at a birthday party when the clown just announced he was going to make balloon animals. She was practically hosing the mare down and scrapping the water off her at the same time.

I never saw her so animated and happy. I actually didn't know that she enjoyed riding and thought it was just something her parents had forced her to do.

"Do you think it went well," she asked.

"Yes."

"Did I look good on her?"

"Wonderful."

"Will I be riding her again or another of your horses?"

"Her."

She sighed in relief. "He's very good, isn't he?"

"Lockie?"

"Yes! He didn't yell at me once."

"He wouldn't do that. He's a wonderful teacher; very knowledgeable and perceptive."

"I felt relaxed. Did I look relaxed?"

"You looked like you could have fallen asleep," I replied.

"Is he staying?"

"Who?"

"Lockie."

"Yes."

"Why?" Rogers asked.

"Excuse me?"

"Didn't your father bring him on board to get Greer to the National Horse Show? She's not going so why would he stay here?"

"Rogers. We have a lovely farm."

"I know but he's so much better than . . . oops."

"Better than teaching Greer and me?"

Rogers grabbed my arm. "I didn't mean it like that! I meant he could be at international level."

"Right now he's going to get Greer ready for the jumper division on the Winter Circuit. That's a huge project and Lockie wants to do it. He likes it here. His horse is here now and he's settling in."

Tracy came in, unclipped the mare and brought her back to her stall as I walked out of the barn with Rogers.

"His horse is here? Which one?"

I stopped in front of Wingspread.

"Oh my God. That's the most beautiful horse I've ever seen."

"Yes, he's very attractive and I'll tell Lockie you said so."

We went out into the sun and Rogers opened the door to her car. "What about you? What are you going to be doing now that Butch is retired?"

"Lockie's been trying to teach me a little about dressage. It gives him something to do when he's not doing something more important."

"Then you don't have to jump."

"Exactly."

Rogers got into her car.

"I'll see you Wednesday."

"See you."

"Thanks, Talia."

I waved goodbye. She shouldn't thank me yet. If she knew what I was planning, she might not even come back.

When I reached the terrace, Lockie and Jules were at the table, working on some of her should-be-famous cold eggplant appetizer. They smiled as I went inside to clean up.

I came back out, sat and Jules dished out some eggplant for me.

"We're having grilled panini for lunch. Is everyone happy with that?"

"Very," Lockie replied. "What is it?"

"An Italian pressed sandwich," I said.

"Why would you press it? Is it wrinkled? Would it be embarrassed to go out in public looking so slovenly?"

I laughed.

"To blend the flavors," Jules explained.

"A normal sandwich is too simple around here," he said.

"Yes, it is," Jules replied as she went into the kitchen.

"What's this plan you have?"

Saved by the UPS man. The brown truck stopped by the walkway and Tom got out carrying a large box.

"Hi, Talia. I don't know who this is, but it's your address. Lockie Malone?"

"That would be me," Lockie said.

"Hi," Tom replied as he put the box on the table. "Running late today. Say hi to Jules for me. See you."

"Bye."

"I didn't order anything," Lockie pointed out as he removed his utility knife from his back pocket.

"I did."

"Of course you did," he said slicing open the box and lifting the box inside to the table then opening it. "What is it, Tali?"

"Unsweetened coconut water."

"I've never heard of it."

"It's very hydrating. I don't see you carrying around a water bottle."

"It's like a baby and their baba."

"You should. It's summer. People need water."

He gave me a look.

"If you don't take in enough fluids . . . you know all this from horse shows! Any horse outside in the summer must have access to water. You're not an exception to the rule. You must maintain your electrolytes. If you're not going to take care of yourself, I'll force you to."

He removed a large can from the case and read the label.

"You'll keep them in the refrigerator and a couple times a day you'll have one. I'll make sure there is a supply of bottled water in there, too."

"You just want to catch me peeing behind the barn."

"Not hardly. Why can't men use the bathroom like a normal person?"

"You mean normal as in like a girl?"

"Okay."

"Yeah, I don't think so."

Jules returned to the terrace with a tray of sandwiches and accompaniments. "Are we arguing?"

I looked at Lockie.

"No," he said.

We ate lunch while Jules told us about her last trip to Italy and all the wonderful food she'd had in tiny trattorias throughout the countryside. I wished we were going to Italy instead of Los Angeles in the fall because I loved spending time with her and considered her my big sister.

"I made some lemon ice for dessert. Is anyone interested?"

"Of course."

"Then I'll go get it and you can go back to arguing," Jules said as she returned to the house.

"We weren't arguing," Lockie said to me.

"No."

"When you tell me this plan concerning Rogers, are we going to start?"

I laughed. "I hope not. You can say no and my feelings won't be hurt."

"What would hurt your feelings?"

"So many things. A huge list." That was true and there was no sense in going there. "Here's my idea. Rogers is a good rider with no confidence. Point and go with the mare."

"Yes. I'm starting to not like it already."

Jules put down two dishes of ice in front of us with wafer cookies on the side and went back in the house.

"It gets better. You're switching me to dressage. Switch Rogers to combined training. She used to hunt. Going cross country isn't a problem for her as long as she's not on Sinjon. Start her in the Novice division and let her go."

"I don't know. Combined training is a far cry from equitation."

"She's jumping that height already in hunter over fences. She's jumped higher than that with the County Hounds Hunt Club. She'll be fine."

"Yeah, she'll be fine except Rogers is one hundred percent clueless about dressage."

"If you let her, Rogers would rest her head on your boot," I said.

"Excuse me?"

"She's got a thing for you."

"What kind of thing?"

"Didn't you see her blushing and practically whispering every time she had to speak to you?" I asked.

"Please tell me you would tease Butch like this and you're not serious."

"I do tease him but, this is for real."

"Now I have to teach Rogers who is afraid of her horse and has a crush on me and Greer who wants to . . . God, I don't know what she wants to do to me."

"Isn't that the exciting part for men?"

Lockie finished his dessert and pushed back from the table. "Yeah, no. What do we have to do to get Greer to keep her pants on?"

"Worry about keeping your own pants on."

~ 20 ~

HE BEGAN WALKING ACROSS THE TERRACE. "You mean I'm not expected to service you two mares?"

I stood up and headed back to the barn with him. "It's not in the job specs."

"That's a relief."

We walked down the driveway.

"I was wondering something about you."

"Don't wonder, just ask."

"When is the last time you had sex," I asked.

"Gee, Tali. Why would you be wondering about that?"

"You don't have to answer."

"Why would you even be thinking about it?" Lockie asked then paused. "No, don't tell me, let me imagine the reason. Hmm Hmmm Hmmm."

"What are you imagining?"

"Day One it's like King Stud coming out of the van. Ears up, tail like an unfurled flag in the wind, nostrils flaring, neck arched. He can smell the mares. He snorts. He paws the ground. He's not confused, he knows what his job is and he's ready to do it."

I closed my eyes. "I'm sorry I asked."

"Are you really sorry?"

"Oh yeah."

Lockie stopped laughing. "On my own or with someone else?"

"Both."

"The answer to part a is the last time I tried, Lockie was saying to me 'Not tonight, dear, I have a headache.' The answer to part b is I don't remember."

"You don't remember in what way?"

"In the way that I don't remember some things about my life before the accident. Blank. It's just not there anymore. I obviously didn't have a girlfriend because no one showed up at the hospital and no one has come around to yell at me for ignoring her since."

"Well, there is Alise."

"I don't remember her."

We continued to the barn.

"When's the last time you had sex," he asked. "Was it with Josh?"

"He's gay."

160

"He could have tried."

"Not with me he wouldn't."

"Maybe he isn't King Stud but Princeling Stud-in-Training."

"Josh is a nice boy."

"That's very sweet. Would you tell Butch?" Lockie asked.

"No."

"Would you tell me?"

"No."

"I told you."

"You'd tell everyone. You're a guy," I replied.

"I'm glad you noticed!"

"Yes, I noticed."

"What does that have to do with it?"

"Guys brag about sex."

"Yeah. I have a lot to brag about in that department. Failure to launch and I can't remember."

"Did you tell the doctor?"

"I told you."

We were almost at the barn and I stopped walking. "Lockie?"

"What, Tali?" He stopped alongside me.

I didn't know if I should tell him. There was so much I kept to myself since my mother died. I valued Rogers as a friend, but didn't trust her to keep a secret. I loved Jules but there were things she didn't need to know. I would never tell

Josh; we weren't that close. The isolation at the farm left me with Butch as my confident. He would never tell.

I took a deep breath. "I don't trust men."

"I know."

I didn't know how to reply.

"Was that so hard to say?"

"Yes."

He began walking again. "You can't unsay it. Tack up CB and put your helmet on and we'll go for a ride."

"Who's CB?" I asked following him into the barn.

"The Chrysler Building horse."

"Lockie," I protested.

"Give the guy a break. Joy? You're going to call him Joy in front of his friends and family?"

"He doesn't have any family here."

"We're his family now," Lockie slid Wing's stall door open. "You want him to be embarrassed in front of Butch?"

It had never occurred to me. "Do you think he would be?"

"I would be. Butch. That's a man's name. Joy. That's a girl's name. Always name a horse something they will live up to."

"His name is Joyful Spirit." I looked down the aisle and could see his grey nose poking out between the bars.

"Then it's his show name, not his stable name."

"I like Joy."

"I do, too, it works great on dishes and rinses off so fast."

Lockie walked Wing out of the stall and put him on the cross ties. "Are you coming with me or am I going by myself?"

Ten minutes later, we were hacking through an empty field since all the horses were inside during a summer afternoon.

"So you think Rogers can do a dressage test, ride cross-country and complete the stadium jumping phase."

"Yes."

Lockie turned to me. "I only have two hands. If I have to hold your hand and Greer's hand, I can't hold Rogers' hand, too."

"I'm not going to be doing anything, why do you have to hold my hand?"

"Maybe I want to," Lockie said and looked up and down the length of the stone wall facing us. "Where's the gate?"

I pointed to the bottom of the pasture.

"I'm not going all the way down there. That's a waste of time."

A moment later, Wing was galloping toward the wall.

"Don't!"

In one immense leap, Wing flew over the wall and Lockie pulled up on the far side.

"Why are you still over there?" He called to me.

"Are you insane?"

"No."

I sat on CB, not moving.

"Come on, Tali. Jump him over the wall."

I shook my head.

"I can't hear your head rattle from here."

"No. It's crazy."

"Point, kick and hold onto his mane if you have to. He'll take care of the rest."

"No."

"Are you telling me you came out here year after year and you didn't ever jump Butch over this wall?"

"Did you hear me tell you that?"

"So you did?"

"No, I didn't."

"Talia. It's hot out here, let's get in the woods where it's cool." He dropped the reins and held up his hands. "Only got two of them. One's yours." He pointed at me.

I took a breath, closed my legs on CB's sides and pointed him at the wall. A moment later, we were on the other side.

"Easy," Lockie said.

"You scared me!"

He looked at me in surprise. "You're serious?"

"Of course!"

"You jumped him before. You get along really well together. He's so athletic, this was nothing for him."

"For you!" I was furious.

"What about me?"

"You could have been hurt. You can't afford to take

chances like that. You don't jump fences when you don't know what's on the other side. What if there were rocks from the wall fallen on the ground or old rusty farm equipment?"

Lockie was startled. "This is about me?"

"Of course it's about you."

"Tali. Calm down. It's okay."

"It's not okay."

He leaned over and put his hand on my leg. I pushed it off with my hand.

"Learn to trust me. I don't ride a course without walking it first."

"You were out here?"

"Yes. I've walked all the trails and all the fields. I haven't gone up the mountain yet."

All my fears from the past were threatening to tsunami me. "You have to be more careful."

"I can't live like that."

"You can't have another accident. The doctor doesn't even want you riding."

"I can only promise you one thing. I will be as careful as I can be. Okay?"

"No."

"Would you lock Butch in his stall?"

"To keep him safe? Yes."

"And if every day he became more sad, seeing CB

rolling in the grass and the ponies chasing after each other and all he could do was try to see down the aisle to watch someone get brushed and listen to the wrong station on the radio?"

"But that's not his life. He does go outside."

"And I've got bad news for you. Last night he was out there running around without permission."

I didn't realize he was carousing after I went to sleep. "Maybe he shouldn't go in the field, maybe he should only go in the paddock."

"Where he'll pace the fenceline. And if you keep him in the stall, he'll start to pace in there and it won't be pretty. You can't control everything, Tali. You don't have to."

My throat tightened and I couldn't speak for a long moment. "She should still be alive."

"Yes. I'm sorry you miss her so much. To have so many people love her, and continue to think so fondly of her, tells me she must have been wonderful."

"She was."

"Your mother gave you life so you could enjoy it. Don't disappoint her."

"She would want me to take care of you."

"You do. And she'd be very proud of the way you've become such a remarkable young woman but she'd know I have to live my life even if that means taking some risks. Tali, few people have an accident like mine and survive it.

Now with so much to live for, I don't want to let anything get by me."

I did understand but to live recklessly after a second chance was to be ungrateful. "Can we negotiate it?"

"We'll find a middle ground."

"Can my father negotiate for me? He's better at it."

"No, this is between us. What's a middle ground?" Lockie thought as we rode up the hill to the woods. "I won't jump anything over four feet."

"I do not agree to that at all."

"Four feet, that's my final offer."

"Final? That's your first offer. What's negotiation about that? You tell me and I'm supposed to say yes?"

"I'm very persuasive."

"Okay. Four feet."

Lockie turned to me in amazement.

"When the doctor says yes to three," I added.

The doctors didn't want him riding at all and said yes to flat work just because he was so persuasive. They would never give the green light to jumping.

"You drive a hard bargain. All right."

"But you're not competing."

"Jumper, not cross country."

"No."

"I'll change your mind."

"No, you won't."

"We'll see."

And with that, they were galloping up the hill with CB and me trying to keep up.

— 21 —

"I CAN'T HAVE A LESSON IN THE AFTERNOON." CB and I jogged around the indoor.

"Why not?"

"Because I'm going to the theater."

"John Barrymore is performing at the local playhouse?"

"Josh."

"That's right. Josh. No."

"Excuse me?"

"I don't want you to go."

"Lockie, Josh is . . ."

"An old friend. Still no."

"Why?"

"Because you're not his beard anymore."

"He hasn't come out to his parents yet."

"That's not your problem. Inside leg at the girth, Talia."

Using Lockie's dressage saddle, I felt like I was riding western, it was so different from what I accustomed to. The flap was much longer, the seat much deeper. Trying to get CB to curve his body around my leg was an exercise in futility.

"Get off, I'll show you."

"Lock . . . no."

Striding over, long legs covering the ground from the middle of the ring to the track with no effort, he stood at CB's head and I slid off.

"Do you want a leg up?"

"I think I can do it." He was in the saddle in one smooth movement.

"What about a helmet?"

"I'm going once around the outside. I can manage without bubble wrap."

"I'm registering a protest."

"Fine. Remember, it's shoulder-in not head in. Both hands slightly to the inside. Slightly. Use your fingers on the reins. Don't fight him, keep the jaw supple."

Without bothering to adjust the leathers, he rode without stirrups. Lockie put CB into a collected trot and demonstrated. "Inside leg at the girth, not behind it. You don't want to push the hindquarters. Don't lean your body into the center of the ring. Stabilize with the outside rein."

It was basic dressage. Of course, Lockie could do it. Of course, CB could do it. Of course, I couldn't.

Lockie pulled CB back into a walk.

"Since you're up there, would you do an extended trot?" I asked.

"I thought you wanted me on the ground and now you want me to show off."

"Half way around."

CB picked up a trot and a few strides later was extending his front legs fully out in front. It was breath-taking. He went from being a patient school horse, to an upper level dressage horse because I got off and Lockie got on.

Pulling up, they walked over to me and Lockie slid off. "Okay. You do it."

"I'm never going to be able to do it," I said.

"That's the spirit! Quit right at the beginning. Leg up in three."

"So we'll have the lesson in the morning tomorrow."

"I'm going to the city for a doctor's appointment. Go do a shoulder-in."

"So it's a day off for both of us."

"No, it's not a day off for you. Come out here and work. Have Rogers come over and help her. I'll come home and we'll go to the play together."

"Lockie."

"Talia," he said mimicking me. "Too much outside rein. Please pay attention to what you're doing."

"Then quit talking to me."

"Quit arguing with me and say yes."

"Yes."

"Terrific. Inside leg. There you go. You've got it."

"Shoulder-in or giving in?"

"Both."

* * *

I was a nervous wreck every time he went to the doctor. The lesson learned from the last years with my mother was that with each doctor's appointment we were told her condition had deteriorated. This was a completely different situation, I was aware of that, but, emotionally, it felt the same.

At nine a.m., getting on CB, I rode in the outdoor arena while Tracy managed the barn chores. CB had this little swish thing he would do with his rear end. I could feel the movement under me but had never seen him do it. It felt like he was pleased with himself and that's how he expressed it.

After twenty minutes, I gave his neck a pat as we left the ring and went for a walk. I needed to build a relationship with CB but felt untrue to Butch at the same time. We had been through so much together and Butch really had been my best friend; I wasn't sure how many best friends I could have without my attention being diluted.

When we returned to the barn, Rogers was tacked and ready to go. It was an easy decision to make to stay on CB, if it had been Butch, I would have stayed on him.

Rogers got on the mare and walked up to us. "He's huge."

"He's a big boy," I patted him without thinking about it. That was a good thing.

We went into the outside ring and I had Rogers do what Lockie would have asked her to practice. She was becoming more relaxed with each session and jumped the fences left over from Greer's last lesson on Spare. They weren't as substantial as the ones Counterpoint would have schooled over but Spare wasn't as far along.

Rogers was smiling broadly when we finished.

"Want to take a little trail ride?"

"Could we?"

"Sure, why not?"

"Does she know about trails? Will she be okay?"

"She'll be fine. Drop your reins and go for a hack."

"Drop the reins!" Rogers was on the brink of a major panic.

"I guess you never did that with Sinjon."

"He'd run away with me."

Poor Rogers.

"Karneval won't."

I dropped the reins on CB's neck to the buckle. "No problem. These are not Thoroughbreds; they're not as tightly wound as some of them."

If I were to be perfectly honest, Wingspread was a Thoroughbred and didn't exhibit any of the temperament I would have expected from a horse that looked as magnificent as he. Lockie had done a fantastic job training him.

I glanced at my watch. He probably wouldn't be out of the doctor's office for at least an hour. My phone was in my back pocket since I had insisted he call the moment he was heading home.

"Where's Greer?" Rogers asked as we headed toward the woods.

"She went to Misquamicut with Sabine and her family. It's one of the last weekends she'll be able to go to the beach before school starts."

"What about Counterpoint?"

"Derry Friel comes twice a week to school him and Greer almost always manages to find time to ride two more times."

"I thought she was excited about having a new horse."

"She is and she's excited about Lockie but it's summer."

"I forgot."

The less Greer was around, the happier I was. In a few weeks, she'd be back in her room down at the end of the hall, annoying me every night.

"I've been wondering," Rogers started. "Lockie found a buyer for Sans Egal, do you think he could find one for Sinjon?"

"He probably could but then you wouldn't have a horse."

"Is Karneval for sale?"

"I don't know," I replied truthfully.

Lockie and I had discussed Rogers riding the mare with the intention of getting some mileage and publicity and then selling her. Did it matter if she was sold now for less than she would bring later? It was Lockie's barn to run.

"Have you thought this through," I asked.

"Yes."

"Where would you keep her? I don't think Robert would tolerate you leaving him, buying a horse from us and keeping it there."

"Can't I keep Karneval here?"

"We don't board horses," I said.

"I'm your friend," Rogers protested.

"You are. This isn't my decision to make. It's primarily up to my father because it's his farm, his barn and his insurance."

"You'll ask?"

Rogers was practically begging.

"I love this horse. If I can't keep her here, how can I ride with Lockie?"

She loved her?

"Enough. I'll ask. I thought your parents liked Sinjon. They paid a lot of money for him."

The horses splashed into the stream and stopped for a drink of water.

"But I didn't make it to the finals so what's the point anymore? They can't brag about me to the members of the country club."

"I'm sorry."

There had to be so much pressure on her and every lesson on Sinjon with Robert screaming at her had to be torture. For the very first time, my father seemed the better parent. He did want us to excel but I never remember being berated when we didn't.

Of course, that was probably because he couldn't get a word in edgewise with Greer screaming at the top of her lungs that she had been cheated once again.

Finally, this fall, she would be competing and not being judged. Either Counterpoint would drag her over the fences for clean rounds or not. And, if not, my bet was that Lockie would simply go out and find a horse that could get the job done.

After about a half hour walk through the woods until we couldn't bear the deer flies a moment longer, we returned to the barn. Rogers pampered, petted and fed Karneval carrots until there was nothing left to do but go home. I walked her out to the car and waved goodbye.

At least the horse would have a good home, for a while. I always worried about their futures. If we sold Karneval to Rogers, she'd be a wonderful owner but what happened if Rogers had to go to college and didn't have time for horses. The next owner might not be so nice.

CB, Butch, the ponies and, as far as I was concerned, Wingspread, were never leaving Bittersweet Farm. They would live in the lap of equine luxury forever.

Jules and I were finishing lunch in the kitchen when my cell phone rang. It was Lockie. I clicked it on. "Hi."

"Hi."

"Bottom line it. Are you okay?"

"Yes, Talia. He ran some more tests and decided everything is fine."

Everything was not fine. If he took the prescription and could barely stand up afterwards, that was an indication all was not well. "What about the meds?"

"We're trying a different combination. It'll be okay. I'll be home in two hours. You'll see for yourself nothing is wrong."

"You'll have to be very convincing."

"I will be. What do I have to wear tonight?"

"Wear what you wore to the Standish anniversary party."

"See you."

"Not if I see you first."

"Silly Filly." He clicked off.

Jules put a slice of peach tart with her flakey crust in front of me and sat down with one piece for herself. "I was only able to hear half the conversation but what's going on between you two?"

I shrugged. "Nothing specific."

Jules nodded as she used a large spoon to scoop up the tart and caramel gelato.

"I'm the boss's daughter."

"Yes, you are."

"He likes it here."

"I'm glad he does."

"He finally found a place where he can get better or if this is it and there's no better, Bittersweet is a good place to live. Like with CB, not much will ever be asked of Lockie."

Jules put her hand on my arm. "You are . . ."

"Sshhh. Don't say anything. My mother was but I'm not."

— 22 —

A FEW HOURS LATER the car and driver brought Lockie home and we had dinner in the kitchen. I told him Rogers was begging to buy Karneval but I hadn't known what to say.

"You bought her to sell, didn't you," Jules asked.

"Yes," Lockie replied.

"So sell the horse. Rogers is a nice girl," Jules said.

"The problem is I have two ponies, Butch and CB. Greer has two horses now. Wingspread is here. We only have twelve stalls. If Karneval stays, we only have four stalls left. It doesn't leave us much room to do business."

"I don't know that it's a problem until the middle of winter," Lockie said. "The ponies could stay out in the shed."

"Be serious."

"Ponies? If you put blankets on them they'll be fine. So would CB and Karneval."

I knew he was right but that still meant for the winter months we had limited free space. "The question you need to answer is: are you going to buy and sell horses?"

"I don't have much choice. I owe your father a lot of money."

"For what?" I asked.

"Wingspread."

I shook my head. "I asked my father to buy me the horse. I didn't like him so I gave him to you. You don't owe my father anything."

"I can't accept a gift like that and you know it."

Standing, I went to the pad of paper by the wall phone, picked up the pen and began to write.

"Sold to Lockie Malone one Thoroughbred horse known as Wingspread for $1 and other valuable considerations. Talia Margolin." I signed the paper and passed it over to him. "Done."

Lockie took the paper from me. "I'll still pay you back."

"You're not going to argue about it; you're going out on your first real date! I'm so excited. Go change and come back here and I'll take photos."

"You will not," I said.

Lockie stopped at the door. "Why not? I'm very handsome."

"Not without clover."

"I knew you were fickle but I didn't know to what extent," he replied as he left.

Jules watched him walk off the terrace then turned to me. "I think I'm falling in love with him just a little bit."

"Jules," I groaned.

* * *

An hour later, he was back after showering and changing and Lockie was correct. He was very handsome.

We drove to the next town where the playhouse was located and I filled him in on what Josh had been doing in high school, the plays and auditioning for repertory companies in the summer. This was the first year Josh had experienced any success and I wasn't sure how much the Standishes knew about his desire to act. Josh would go to college, that was a given. A Standish would have to graduate from a very fine school and Josh could minor in performing arts while majoring in finance. They had his life pretty well figured out for him and he'd known that well before high school.

"It's okay to go your own way, Tali," Lockie said when I paused. "You knew there was no future in the relationship. You're still friends. Nothing has changed except you're not pretending anymore."

"You're right. I just . . ."

"Find it hard to let go."

"Yes."

"I know."

He parked my truck under some pine trees at the farthest point from the playhouse and we got out.

"You look very pretty tonight."

"Thank you."

"Did you dress for me or Josh?"

"Lockie. You really can be impossible."

"No, I still am very possible and all you have to do is answer."

"My date is with you. I'm here with you. I dressed for you. Not that Josh didn't help me pick out what clothes to wear on other occasions."

"I'll bet he has excellent style sense."

"It sounds like a joke but he does."

"I'm not joking about it."

The playhouse was a red converted barn and had been a theater for over fifty years. The walls of the lobby were crowded with framed photographs of famous and near-famous actors who had performed there. A landmark in the area, it had a reputation for high-quality productions always written up in the local newspapers and sometimes even the New York Times.

I was certain this appearance would look very good on Josh's resume.

We walked up the steps and entered through the double

doors. Immediately in front of us in the foyer were the Standishes, and they were not happy.

Mrs. Standish crossed to me. "You've broken his heart."

"Excuse me?"

"Josh goes away for two months and you don't even have the common courtesy to break up with him before finding someone new."

"That's not how it was," I replied. I had no idea what Josh had told her and couldn't help but feeling a little hurt being the target of her vehemence. She was protecting her son, but I had been a good friend to him for years. Maybe she had no idea how many times I covered for him. That's what a beard does.

"Since I'm the new man, you should take your problems up with me," Lockie said evenly. "If Josh couldn't hang onto his girlfriend, that's not Talia's fault. Josh is great. But, come on, could he really compete with me? Enjoy the play."

Lockie took my hand and pulled me away from them.

"Stop being stunned," he said as we found our seats. "Did you actually think they'd take this news well?"

"I didn't think. I had other things on my mind." I gave him a look.

"Tali. I'm not a hundred percent; I will never be a hundred percent again, but life is good. Now what the hell are we seeing?"

I handed him the computer printed playbill.

"Oh God, *The Boys In The Band*? The only thing Josh hasn't done is announce it on a billboard. Okay. Wake me when it's over."

"It's about gay men?"

"Yes."

What happened to *The Mousetrap*? "I thought he was going to be in something like *Guys and Dolls*." That seemed to be the kind of play performed at the playhouse each summer.

"This is like that, but think of it as *Guys and Guys*."

The house lights came down and Act One began. Since I wasn't paying attention, I was lost almost immediately. Josh was on stage and speaking his lines, so that was a good thing but beyond that, I had no idea what was going on. It was no comedy.

It would have been nice to get out of the house and see something happy. Maybe with some singing. *Oklahoma!* or *West Side Story*. But this was art. All the actors were showing off their chops and I was bored beyond belief.

The act finished, the curtain closed on the apartment set and I stood.

"Let's så go."

"Are you sure?"

"Yes."

Lockie stood, we made our way to the side exit and left.

"How's Josh going to explain this to his parents?"

"He should try the truth," Lockie replied as he extracted his sunglasses from his pocked and slipped them on.

"Are your eyes bothering you?"

"No, but it's dark, and I don't want to have a problem with oncoming headlights."

"I'll drive."

"Thanks."

We got in my truck and headed for home. My relationship with Josh would never be the same, never as close. That chapter in my life was over.

* * *

"Why is there a light on in the hayloft?" I asked as we drove down the driveway.

Lockie removed his glasses. "Yeah. It's not even bright enough to be an overhead."

I parked at the front entrance and got out. "It doesn't make sense. Maybe Pavel was up there with a flashlight and forgot it?"

We started down the aisle.

"Why don't you stay here and I'll go look." Lockie said.

I took his hand. "There are so many drawbacks to you not being Butch."

"You can't pick out my hooves, so what else?"

"You're sweet." I stepped closer to him and blew a soft breath over his lips.

Just the way Butch would do when I breathed into his nose, Lockie blew a breath back.

"Ready?"

"Yes."

"Have you ever seen anyone in the act before?"

"Not in real life."

— 23 —

"THIS WILL BE VERY REAL."

We walked quietly up the steps to the haymow.

There was a small miner's lamp casting enough light to be able to see. I could hear some movement. It was clear what was going on.

Lockie stopped. "Still sure," he whispered.

"Yes."

We walked past several tons of hay and found them on Counterpoint's monogrammed sheet, which had arrived earlier that day.

Her clothes were strewn over the hay bales.

"Greer meet Derry. Oops. I guess you already met," I said.

Derry stopped what he was doing.

"Good time to dismount," Lockie suggested to him.

Greer looked up and glared at me. "You have lousy timing."

With no graceful way to end this, Derry pushed back, grabbed for Greer's shirt and threw it over her.

There was a bottle of champagne from my father's wine cellar next to them, on its side, empty.

"Do you want me to fire him?" Lockie asked me.

"Is he any good?" I asked.

Derry was on his feet scrambling to pull on his jeans and boots.

"Let's ask Greer," Lockie replied. "You mean on a horse? Yeah, he can get the job done."

Greer tried pushing the hair out of her face, but it was warm in the loft and they had been exerting each other so she was a more than a little damp.

"Then I'm okay with it," I said, picked up the miner's lamp and turned back for the stairs.

Lockie followed me. "Do you think Jules has any of that gelato left?"

"Wouldn't that be good?"

* * *

We sat on the glider on the terrace with our ice cream and not many minutes later Derry drove up the drive in his truck, stopped at the front of the house to let Greer off and then continued into the night.

"I can find someone else," Lockie said.

"She'll get in trouble with that one, too."

"Should your father be told?"

"I think he realized with Rui there was nothing he could do with her anymore."

We went back and forth on the glider, looking at the stars and the lightning bugs.

"I'm going to turn in," Lockie said.

"It's been a long day for you."

"Kiss my muzzle, skip the extra flake of hay and I'll turn myself out."

"You could be a private detective with snooping like that." I often went down to check on Butch and throw him a little bit of hay.

"I like watching you with him. I . . ."

"What?"

"Don't leave CB out. You're not betraying Butch. Love stretches."

He leaned over and I kissed his cheek.

"See you tomorrow, Silly Filly," Lockie said and headed down to the barn.

I went into the house, locked the door turned off the lights and went upstairs to my room.

Greer was sitting on my bed.

"What now?"

Less drunk than earlier but now she was angrier. "Butt out of my life!"

"Sorry."

"You're not!"

"I am. I want to go to sleep and you're screaming."

"My father and I are not like you."

"He's my father, too."

"That was just the luck of the sperm race."

"Shut up, Greer, you're still drunk."

"We want to enjoy life."

"There are lots of way to enjoy life and not all of them involve the prevention of sexually transmitted disease."

She shrieked at me.

"I hope you were using protection, I didn't get that good of a look with the mood lighting."

"I've put up with just about enough from you. You were forced on me six years ago and it's been hell ever since."

"For me, too, sis."

"You can't tell me how to live!"

"I'm not telling you. No one is telling you anything anymore. You can do as you please. Wear Derry out. No one cares."

"Then why did you come into the loft?"

"Duh. Because we were worried about the possibility of a fire starting. There was a light on that shouldn't be there. Use your brains, Greer, instead of relying on another part of your anatomy all the time."

"You are a bitch!"

"Yeah, I know, of the first order."

"You'll pay for this."

"I'd be careful with the threats."

"Are you going to do something to me?" Greer taunted.

"No. Hubris meet Nemesis."

"What does that mean?"

"Look it up. If you mean harm to someone, eventually it'll backfire. That's the way the world works."

"You and your mother with your goody-goody platitudes. My father and I aren't like that. We're practical. We take what we want."

"You extracted the wrong lesson from his life in that case."

Greer stormed out of the room, slamming the door behind her. I went over and locked it to make sure she didn't pay me a surprise visit in the middle of the night.

As much as my father might have wanted my mother, and I believe he did those last years, she held herself back. Even after they married, he never got what he wanted—for her to give herself to him fully.

Sad, really.

* * *

A week later, I was eating breakfast when Greer entered the kitchen, leaned over and whispered into my ear "I can get any man I want and you know who I want?"

~ 24 ~

PICKING UP WHAT WAS LEFT of the half cantaloupe I was eating, I pushed it into her face.

She started shrieking like something bad had happened to her. A moment later, my father appeared from his office, just in time to grab her arm before she began flailing away at me.

"You go to your room," he commanded.

"What are you going to do to her? She attacked me!"

"Be quiet for once. Talia, come into my office."

Jules cleaned up the melon as I started to leave the room.

"Greer should be doing that," I told her.

"Please stop fighting with her."

"Yeah."

Jules hadn't been told we caught Greer and Derry in

mid-ecstasy a week ago. I was hoping it would go away but Greer wouldn't give up. She had been taunting me whenever possible. At the barn, she had been walking her walk and wearing tight tank tops with no bras for Lockie.

For a brief few days, I had thought when school started she would have more on her mind than me.

But it wasn't about me anymore, it was about Lockie. She had to have him. He was like the Medal and the Maclay all rolled into one. He was like winning the Grand Championship of the Sex over Fences division.

I followed my father into his office and he closed the door.

"What's this about?" He sat and pointed at the leather chair on the opposite side of his desk where I sat when brought in for a lecture.

I sat.

His desktop computer was on, there was a laptop on; it was probably something with the stock market. I had no idea what he did in the office.

There was a change in his demeanor. For the first time ever I felt like he was taking sides. He had been so careful over the years trying to treat us equally, that had been plain to me. If I hadn't always been so angry with him, I would have appreciated the even-handedness more.

But I wasn't my mother and I didn't have her guidance to tell me how to behave, I just had to try to imagine what she would have advised. I had no idea what she would say now. Probably being grounded for a while would have been part of it. She thought violence was the last resort when defending yourself, not the first.

But this didn't feel like the first time, it felt as though Greer had been pulling this routine on me for years. There was just something so mean inside her; the capacity for compassion was missing.

Her mother was like that. They were both emotionally cold and calculating. Their first thought always seemed to be "What's in it for me?"

Even though we were related, we couldn't be more dissimilar. We didn't even look like sisters.

"Talia, what's it about this time?"

"Lockie and I went to see Josh at the playhouse and came back early because it was so boring. We saw a light in the loft so went up to make sure it wasn't a fire."

"And found Greer with whom this time?"

"Derry, the rider Lockie hired to school Counterpoint while Greer's on summer vacation."

He snapped the cap back on his fountain pen. "How is Lockie?"

"Better, and thank you for arranging for the doctors and getting him the contact lenses from Singapore."

"Do they help?"

"Very much. He used to be so uncomfortable."

"Do you like your new horse?"

"He's a door opening."

"Your mother used to say that."

I nodded. I remembered it very well. All doors are locked except the one God wants you to go through.

"She would be proud of you."

"She judged me favorably." Too favorably from what I could tell.

"Your mother was a very unique individual but so are you. I will try to talk some sense into Greer."

I had tried to leave Greer to her own choices and let her misbehaviors surface own their own. Tattling would have gotten me nowhere and taken up a good part of my life to boot. Telling my father anything was not something I chose to do over the years. She was his daughter and he had feelings for her even if I didn't. Only if asked, did I say anything.

"Greer wants to . . ." I couldn't bring myself to say the words "with Lockie."

"No, that's not a good idea."

"Is her mother like this?"

"Exactly."

"You don't owe me an explanation, but why?"

My father exhaled. "Because I didn't understand intimacy until I met your mother and by then Victoria had already happened."

I could see the horses in the pasture through his windows; they would be coming in soon. "My mother showed me a photo of my grandmother at a resort in the Catskills."

"She showed me that vacation picture, too."

"It was a lesson."

"It was."

* * *

When I got down to the barn, Greer was in the indoor on Counterpoint arguing with Lockie. I stood at the doorway and watched.

"Greer, are you going to do what I ask you to do this morning or not?"

"Not when it goes against my better judgment," she snapped.

"Fine. The session is over for today." Lockie crossed the arena and left by the side door.

She turned and saw me standing at the front entrance. "Bitch!"

"What did I have to do with it?"

"You're turning him against me."

"You did that on your own," I replied and walked back to the barn.

I found him in the feed room opening a bag of Calf Manna. "Does she always have her period?" Lockie asked.

I started to laugh.

He poured the pellets into a metal garbage can, then put the cover down. "Let's go."

"Where?"

"There must be a diner or a café in town."

"Yeah, there's a place near the Green, The Grill Girl. They have good handmade hamburgers."

"Perfect. I'm starving."

We were getting into his truck as Greer was riding Counterpoint back to the barn.

"You were serious?" She shouted.

"I don't know how you treated everyone else who came here to help you but you won't treat me with disrespect," Lockie said and got in the driver's side.

Greer slid off Counterpoint and pulled him over to the truck so she could speak through the window. "I apologize."

"That's very nice."

"That bi . . . Talia attacked me this morning. I was upset with her and took it out on you. That was very wrong of me and I'm sorry."

"We'll take a couple days off."

"I have a show coming up," Greer said sharply.

"Maybe you'll be ready and maybe you'll miss it," Lockie replied. "Please put your horse away or let Tracy do it."

Lockie started the engine and backed the truck slowly away from Greer.

We headed up the driveway.

"She can't have you fired," I said to him.

Lockie stopped at the end of the driveway. "I'm not worried about it, don't you be."

* * *

Greer was on her best behavior at dinner but no one believed it for a minute. She could be quite tolerable and knew how to hold a pleasant conversation. To move in society circles was an expected skill and Greer had acquired it at a young age from her mother.

"Mr. Swope," Lockie began.

"Andrew, please," my father replied.

"Andrew. Rogers called me earlier and made an offer on the German mare, Karneval."

"She can't be serious!" Greer said with a laugh.

Lockie ignored her. "I don't know what your intentions are so before saying anything, I thought it was better to ask."

"It's your barn to run as you see fit."

"There are some complications," Lockie said.

"There always are," my father replied as he took a drink from his wine glass.

"Rogers had a falling out with her trainer and would like to ride with me and keep the horse with us."

"I don't want her here," Greer said.

We all glared at her.

"That dumpy thing? She can barely stay on a horse." Greer glanced around the table. "Why is everyone looking at me? It's true."

"You're being unkind," Jules said evenly.

"What's the problem with the horse staying?" My father asked.

"Perpetual embarrassment," Greer said.

"We'll have one less stall available," Lockie replied without looking at her. "I had been planning on being in Florida for most of the winter but now I'm not sure."

Greer dropped her fork onto her plate. "I thought I was riding the jumper circuit."

"I thought so, too," Lockie replied evenly. "But that would mean you, not Derry, would be riding your horse now. I'm not dragging you and two horses fifteen hundred miles, wasting your father's money on a fool's errand."

Greer stared at Lockie in shock. No one had spoken like that to her. Ever.

My father smiled. "I guess that's settled. What's for dessert?"

Greer shrieked, pushed back from the table, knocking over her water glass and hurried into the house.

"Watermelon granita and stone fruit tart," Jules replied.

"That sounds wonderful."

By the time I helped clear the dinner dishes and serve dessert, Greer was tearing off up the driveway in her Porsche.

"It's always such a relief when she leaves," I said.

Since no one replied, I understood that no one disagreed.

— 25 —

THE FOLLOWING MORNING I was on CB doing a volte, a precise circle, at a collected trot.

"What's he doing?" Lockie asked.

"Nothing. Trotting."

"No, he just did something."

I missed returning to the track at the point where we left it.

"Talia, you missed the marker."

"I can't talk and concentrate at the same time."

"Try harder."

"You asked about his swish."

"Walk."

I pulled CB to a walk.

"What are you talking about?"

"He has this thing he does. I can feel it. I call it his swish."

"Stop him from doing it."

"Yeah. Right away." It came out wrong and I knew it the moment the words left my mouth.

"Excuse me, Miss Margolin?" He was annoyed.

"How do you propose I stop him? He's happy with himself. Maybe he even likes me although God knows I haven't given him very many reasons to do so."

"He shouldn't be happy and pleased with himself, he should be working. Get him to focus."

From the moment he had come down the stairs wearing his glasses an hour ago, I knew that Lockie didn't feel well. He wouldn't be so impatient, nor call me Miss Margolin, if he didn't have a headache. I thought it was a hangover from last night's performance by Greer. It was too much tension for all of us.

He had left the house right after dinner and just as it became dark outside and the horses had been checked for the final time, the lights went off in his apartment.

"I'll try harder," I said.

"We're done for the day."

"I'm sorry."

"I have to take my truck to the mechanic in town."

"Okay. I'll follow you down and bring you back then we can go pick it up later."

"No, Tracy is going with me. Rogers is buying Karneval

and wants you to go Runnymeade with her and pick up her tack. Easton won't give her any grief if you're there."

"Is he selling Sinjon for her?"

"I got him sold to the Bancrofts up in Massachusetts."

I was having a difficult time understanding how this was all working out. "You never saw him."

"That wasn't necessary. They did. They know the horse. I was just the agent. So you can do that?"

"Yes."

"Good."

"When will you be back?"

"Long before you will be, why?"

"I thought maybe we could go for a hack, if you feel like it."

"Maybe later, maybe this evening."

He was giving himself more than six hours to feel better. Perhaps I expected too much of modern medicine, thinking there would be a real abatement of his pain. It hadn't been true for my mother so I was rather naïve imagining this time it would be different.

"Okay."

Before I had even untacked CB, Lockie had driven away in his truck followed by Tracy in hers.

* * *

I was with Rogers for hours, and no, my being there didn't prevent Robert Easton from verbally attacking her. We hadn't even reached the tack room to get her trunk and already she was in tears. That didn't slow him down one iota.

Telling him to go to hell where he was sure to find many compatible friends seemed like the perfect thing to say but only if I wanted to alienate Rogers' former trainer completely. Lockie was certain to have to deal with Easton at some point and this was bad enough, my adding to it wouldn't improve the situation.

I dropped Rogers off at her house after spending an hour trying to calm her down and convince her that the worst was over. She never had to ride Sinjon or be humiliated in a lesson again. Everything had changed in her favor.

Provided Greer shut up and didn't start in on her.

There had to be a solution to the Greer problem, but I had no idea what it was. She had been given two wonderful horses and an opportunity to restart her riding career in a new division. Instead, she had spent most of the summer at the beach or in Millbrook poolside with her friends from school.

What she said she wanted had changed again. She had talked about little else besides the finals for the last two years.

Now she wanted Lockie.

She may have missed the blue ribbon but the one thing Greer never missed was acquiring a designated male target. When Greer said she took what she wanted, that wasn't a boast, that was her track record.

Greer inherited that talent from my father and her mother. Some would call her a lucky girl. I thought she was a slut.

It was two p.m when I pulled my truck in front of the barn and stopped. Lockie's truck wasn't there. He wasn't in the barn. Wingspread was in his stall. I gave Butch a handful of grain and then went to CB's stall to give him a handful.

He nickered as I started to slide the door open. It made me feel guilty for not being more friendly toward him.

This was a new barn, a new home, a new country and I rode him for twenty minutes a day as if he was a bicycle.

Holding out my hand, he ate the grain; I put my arms around his neck, promised to do better and meant it. He pressed down on me with his head and neck like a hug.

Closing the stall door, I wondered if Lockie still had the headache from this morning. I wished that bringing him a handful of grain could make up for the uncomfortable dressage lesson of this morning.

I went up the stairs to his apartment and knocked on the door. "Lockie."

"Sshh!" It was a female voice on the other side of the door. It was Greer.

"It's Talia," I said, louder.

"Don't get up," Greer said, just loud enough for me to hear. "You don't want her to know we're in bed together.

Just be quiet. She'll go away." After a moment, there was giggling.

I tried the doorknob. The door was locked.

For more about Bittersweet Farm, check out *Joyful Spirit* and *Wingspread*, available from Amazon and other other online retailers.

Bittersweet Farm 2: *Joyful Spirit*

Talia Margolin doesn't want to be judged and quickly learns the show ring isn't the only place she'll be tested.

The challenges Talia face now that Lockie Malone is the trainer at Bittersweet Farm stack up like cord wood. Her half-sister, Greer, is making the transition to jumper rider more easily than Talia can switch to dressage. Talia's former boyfriend, Josh, grows closer to Lockie and confides secrets he won't share with her. Then there's the hunter pace looming ahead. Talia wonders if her life can get more difficult.

Does it?

Bittersweet Farm 3: *Wingspread*

"Surprise!" Greer's mother says with her unannounced arrival. What Victoria Swope is doing in town is a mystery but they quickly find out and no one is pleased.

When Greer demands to be home-schooled with Talia, the lessons at Bittersweet Farm aren't restricted to dressage, cross-country, and show jumping. If the half-sisters can't get along, one of them will be sent abroad to finish high school. Unable to bear leaving the farm's trainer, Lockie Malone, or her horse, CB, Talia grits her teeth and tries to move forward.

It's soon obvious that everyone at the farm faces changes and challenges. Solving them is difficult and maybe impossible.

Sign up for our mailing list and be among the first to
know when the next Bittersweet Farm book
will be out.
Send your email address to:

barbara@barbaramorgenroth.com
Note: all email addresses are kept strictly confidential

About the Author

Barbara Morgenroth was born in New York City but now lives somewhere else. She got her first horse when she was eleven and rode nearly every day for many years, eventually teaching equitation and then getting involved in eventing.

Although Barbara started her writing career with tween and YA books, she wound up writing for grown-up daytime television for several years. She then wrote a couple of cookbooks and a nonfiction book on knitting, after which she returned to fiction and wrote romantic comedies.

When digital publishing became a possibility, Barbara leaped at the opportunity and has never looked back. In addition to the fifteen traditionally published books she wrote, Barbara has something in digital format to appeal to almost every reader—from the Bad Apple series and the Flash series for mature YAs, to contemporary romances like *Love in the Air* published by Amazon/Montlake, along with *Unspeakably Desirable*, *Nothing Serious*, and *Almost Breathing*.

10818968R00129

Made in the USA
San Bernardino, CA
26 April 2014